STONE CLIFF SERIES : LOVE LESSONS & WRAPPED UP

CATHRYN FOX

COPYRIGHT

Copyright 2020 by Cathryn Fox
Published by Cathryn Fox
Love Lessons and Wrapped Up

ALL RIGHTS RESERVED. Without limiting the rights under copyright reserved above, no part of this publication may be reproduced, stored in or introduced into a retrieval system, or transmitted, in any form, or by any means (electronic, mechanical, photocopying, recording, or otherwise) without the prior written permission of both the copyright owner and the above publisher of this book.

This is a work of fiction. Names, characters, places, brands, media, and incidents are either the product of the author's imagination or are used fictitiously. The author acknowledges the trademarked status and trademark owners of various products referenced in this work of fiction, which have been used without permission. The publication/use of these trademarks is not authorized, associated with, or sponsored by the trademark owners.

This e-book is licensed for your personal enjoyment only.

This e-book may not be re-sold or given away to other people. If you would like to share this book with another person, please purchase an additional copy for each recipient. If you're reading this book and did not purchase it, or it was not purchased for your use only, then please return to your favorite e-book retailer and purchase your own copy. Thank you for respecting the hard work of this author.

Discover other titles by Cathryn Fox at www.cathrynfox.com. Please sign up for Cathryn's Newsletter for freebies, ebooks, news and contests: https://app.mailerlite.com/webforms/landing/c1f8n1

ISBN 9781989374122

LOVE LESSONS

1

Grace Bennett, creator of the comic strip, *Kate Can't Date*, crumpled up the sheet of paper in front of her and grumbled under her breath as she tossed it into her overflowing trashcan. As it fell out and rolled across the floor of her cubicle—or rather, the floor of her pod, since she considered herself and everyone else who worked behind those ugly orange wall partitions as pod people—she recalled the staff's morning editorial meeting and how her boss, Audrey, had singled her out.

Next week's comic strip has to be about falling in love. Your characters need to grow up, Grace. Instead of writing about funny things that happen on dates, I want you to write about endearing things that happen in love. Next week's Valentine's issue is the perfect time for Kate Can't Date *to take the next step into adulthood.*

Valentine Schmalentine!

If there was one thing Grace couldn't write—or draw—about, it was couples falling in love, which was why her comic strip was a satirical take on dating and mating. After all, one had to write about what one knew, right? And here in Deerfield, Alberta, where the pickings were slim to none, she was more likely to run into a moose at her favorite nightclub than the love of her life—which made it rather difficult to write about the adorable little things that supposedly happened between two people in love.

Damn. Damn. Damn.

She grabbed another sheet of paper and tried again. When she looked at her lame attempt to draw love, what she saw was some idiot standing on Kate's doorstep, holding a wilted bouquet of flowers and a half-eaten box of chocolates. She gave an exaggerated sigh and gazed out her small sliver of an office window, thankful she actually had one in her pod.

Cold February wind whistled outside, blowing up a light dusting of snow in front of her frosty pane. Hugging herself to ward off a chill, Grace stared off into the distance and caught sight of Stone Cliff Resort, a vacation destination that beckoned travelers from all over the world. Fresh stock came in daily at Stone Cliff, all dressed in tight ski pants and ready to hit the slopes. Her fingers drummed on the sleeve of her blouse. Perhaps she should venture up to the lodge to see if she could find true love. Then again, most who vacationed at the resort during Valentine's weekend were either committed couples or newlyweds, and truthfully, if she really wanted to find the right guy, she should probably stop thinking of them as fresh stock.

She glanced up to see her smokin' hot co-worker, who also happened to be her neighbor and very best friend, coming toward her. Grace tapped her pencil on her desk as she watched Mr. Hot Pants himself walk with that easy confidence that drove women wild. Black dress pants hung low on his hips, tightening over hewn thighs with each sexy swagger. His button-down shirt rasped across broad shoulders, showcasing a firm body that had the opposite sex shedding their panties in record time.

Nathan Wright. Nate. Chick bait. Chick bait who knows how to date. Yeah, this was the kind of thing she did when she had writer's block.

Regardless, unlike her, Nate most definitely *did* know how to date. He also knew how to fall in love, which—if the gossip around the water cooler could be believed, not to mention the noises she heard between their paper thin apartment walls—he was known to do every other weekend. Of course, none of those relationships ever lasted very long, but at least he knew how to fall in love and was clearly having great sex. The perma-smile on his handsome face was a true testament to that. Damned if she didn't want to be having hot, break-the-headboard sex, too. The last guy she climbed into bed with went down on her like he was munching on one of Albert's famous prime rib roasts. Cripes, she was about to ask if he needed a knife and fork.

"Hey Gracie," Nate said, as he approached.

She warmed at the lazy yet sexy way her name rolled off his tongue. *Gracie...* She'd always gone by Grace, but for some reason, he was the only guy she ever let get away with cutsey-fying it. Yeah, okay, so she wasn't immune to his charm, either. But they were friends and had been working across the hall from one another at the Gazette since they both gradu-ated university and moved to Deerfield a little over a year ago. For Nate, the oldest of four boys, the small town was home, and his folks still lived in a quaint bungalow the brothers had all grown up in. For Grace, the mountain town was hundreds of miles away from the east coast suburb where she'd grown up, a place she called home, even though it lacked the warmth, comfort, and loving parents most associ-ated with a home.

Nate, on the other hand, had grown up with everything she'd ever wanted, and she often joined him and his family when they all gathered for their big Sunday dinner. They welcomed her with open arms and treated her like she was one of their own. Grace was an only child, and while she loved the camaraderie, teasing jibes, and friendly rivalry among siblings, it also made her long for what he had all that much more. If she ever found herself walking down the aisle—and with the way things were going, she didn't see that happening anytime soon—she'd want it to be with a guy who had what Nate had, so she could have one big crazy-ass family of her own.

Grace and Nate hung out often, but he had never looked at her as anything more than a friend. Then again, there were times he joked about taking her out, but she knew he was teasing. They were good friends, completely at ease with each other, and when they both ended up dateless on a Friday night, as they often did, they usually ended up eating pizza and watching scary movies together. Even though he was more of an action-packed, blow-things-up kind of guy, he always let her have her pick of shows. Probably because he loved watching her get scared so he could tease her. Regardless, she loved horror movies, and he always let her snuggle in to him when something really frightened her.

Now that she thought about it, they'd been hanging out together a lot more often lately—no doubt because she was on a dry spell, and he felt sorry for her. She'd even considered taking him up on his offer to take her out, but didn't want to make things uncomfortable between them, forcing him to spend time with her on an actual date when he wasn't serious. Whenever he asked, she always came back with some smart-assed comment to keep things between them light and easy. Besides, with a little too much junk in her trunk and wiggle in her thighs, she was about as far from his type as a girl could get, which was, she surmised, why he'd never paid her a lick of attention sexually.

Damn. She really wished she hadn't just thought of licking and Nate in the same sentence.

He plunked himself down on the edge of her desk and handed her a much needed mug of coffee.

"Thanks," she said and wrapped her cold hands around the warm mug. She took a sip and released a happy sigh. French vanilla latté with whipped cream, her favorite, and bless Nate for knowing that. Nothing in the world tasted better. Seriously. She flicked her tongue out and licked the cream, and while all that sugary sweetness wasn't helping that thigh situation she'd just lamented over, right now, she didn't care. She had more important things to worry about, like her job.

"You looked like you needed a cup," he said, scrubbing his hand over the sexy scruff on his chin.

She peeked at him over the rim. "What gave it away, the curses rolling down the hall or the pile of crumbled up paper in the trash?"

He leaned close and she caught his scent. Damn the man smelled good—like clean soap, fresh laundry, and something uniquely Nate. The combination of the three brought heat to her face, among other parts of her body.

Needy parts that Nate could sate.

She took another huge drink of her coffee to smother a moan but only ended up burning her damn tongue. But a blister was better than Nate knowing how he truly affected her. Nate thought of her as his asexual friend only, and she didn't want to ruin what they had or cause tension in their relationship by making her interests obvious.

His brow furrowed as those clear blue eyes moved over her face. "You okay?" he asked.

"Just bummed at what Audrey said at the meeting this morning about next week's comic having to be about Kate falling in love." She gave him an exasperated look. "I have no idea what love looks like, so I sure as hell can't draw it."

If only she could do next week's strip on lust. Yeah, she

definitely knew what lust was, considering it was sitting right next to her and staring her in the face. She could whip out a three-page-spread on lust. But best to keep that tidbit to herself, so she shut her mouth and quietly admired Mr. Hot Pants from her chair instead.

He went quiet for a moment, thoughtful, the familiar sexy grin on his gorgeous mouth gone. "I could show you what love looks like," he said softly.

She dropped her paper and was about to burst out laughing when she caught the seriousness in his eyes. *Oh, God.* Serious Nate was ten times sexier! Confused, she set her coffee down and held her hands out at her sides. "How can you possibly teach me anything about love or what it looks like?"

He glanced at the scribbling she'd jotted down moments ago and made a face that suggested she was in a whole lot of trouble. He lifted it from her desk, took a closer look, then shook his head.

"Well, if you think some guy handing a girl half a box of candy and dead flowers on Valentine's is what love looks like, you need more help than I thought."

She snatched the sheet from him and wadded it up into a tight ball. Honestly, how could she know what love looked like? Her mind went back to her upbringing. Her father had left when she was only two, and her mother had been alone ever since, burying herself in her job and paying little attention to the girl that needed her love, affection, and guidance so badly. For as long as Grace could remember, she had done everything on her own and had always taken care of herself. Cripes, no wonder she was so jaded. Without a good role model or personal experiences of love to draw on, she honestly had no idea how to recognize it when she saw it.

"Jesus Nate, you don't have to be so...so honest." She drew back her arm and lobbed the wad of paper toward the trash, the force behind the toss knocking several more out of the can.

He laughed and gave an easy roll of one shoulder. "Sorry," he said. "But I call it as I see it."

"Well, the way I see it, I'm going to be out of a job if I don't figure this out soon."

"Which means you should take me up on my offer and put yourself in my hands, because you obviously need me more than you realize."

Oh, I realize just how much I need you, thank you very much. As far as putting myself in your hands, well...

She pushed back in her chair and folded her arms, ready to hear him out, purely out of curiosity. *Right*, a little voice in the back of her head taunted. "So tell me exactly how you plan to teach me about love."

His sexy grin returned, and she crossed her legs to stop herself from handing him her panties.

"Why don't you leave that up to me," he said.

She arched a brow. "I want to know what you have in mind, Nate."

Naked Nate. Naked Nate on a plate.

Good God, she really needed to grow up or get laid. Or fall in love.

"You give me one week, and I'll teach you all about love," he paused and pointed at her comic strip. "So your Kate will know it when she sees it."

"You know Kate's not real, right?" she said. Then again, who was she kidding? Nate, of all people, likely knew the character in her strip was based on her pathetic love life. And Kate just happened to be her middle name.

His eyes bored into hers, then crinkled at the corners. "Yeah, whatever you say, Gracie. Now do you want my help or not?"

She gave him a skeptical look, wondering how he could possibly help her. "Are you serious?"

"Yes." He paused and angled his head, his gaze moving over her face. "You do trust me, right?"

"Of course," she answered without hesitation. Nate was the one man—the only man—she'd ever trusted.

"Okay, then. Leave it up to me. You know I'll take good care of you."

She nodded, and even though she had no idea what he was up to, if she wanted to learn about love and keep her job, she had no choice but to put herself in his hands.

And let him take care of her, with his hands. And maybe even his tongue.

Oh, God.

He leaned in, so close she could feel his breath against her ear, and whispered, "We'll start tonight. I'll message you the details."

As a fine shiver moved through her, she couldn't help but consider what she was getting herself into, and more importantly, if it involved Nate getting naked.

❷

Nate watched a pretty pink color stain Gracie's cheeks before he pushed off her desk to make his way back to his office. Either she was really excited about his proposal, or he'd just embarrassed the hell out of her. Knowing Gracie and how hard she was to embarrass, he was opting for excited. Opting? Who was he kidding? He was *hoping* for it.

He dropped down into his leather chair and tried to keep the party in his pants to a minimum. But Jesus, talk about fate landing in his lap and giving him the perfect opportunity to finally get closer to the girl he couldn't help but compare every other female to. Gracie. She was sweet, sexy, funny as hell...and refused to go out with him.

They'd met a little over a year ago when they both came to work for the Deerfield Gazette and moved into apartments across the hall from one another. They were friends, good friends, but he'd always felt something more, and in an effort to feel her out, he'd often teased her about going on a date. But she always came back with some witty comment on how she had enough fodder for her comic strip.

Damned if this wasn't the perfect chance to get her to go

out with him, to show her how a woman should really be treated. After watching his folks for years and seeing how they treated one another with kindness and respect, he knew gifts like candy and flowers were nice gestures in a relationship, but real love was about thoughtfulness and putting the other person's needs first. And if things didn't turn intimate after the week was over, if Gracie still didn't see that he was bat-shit crazy about her and reciprocate those feelings, then this little experiment wouldn't jeopardize their friendship. He'd pass off every move he made as helping her cause, because he valued what they had between them too much to ruin it.

He peered out from his partition wall and caught a glimpse of her moving down the hall, that luscious, curvy ass of hers all wrapped up in a sexy pencil skirt, swaying enticingly with each step. He raked his fingers through his hair as he turned his attention to the way her long dark hair swished against her silk blouse—a blouse that did little to hide the way her hard nipples poked against her lace bra. Oh yeah, when the cold air had breezed in through the crack in her window frame, he could see the beautiful outline of her pale buds. A low groan caught in his throat, and he tugged at his collar as his temperature jumped a few degrees.

"Something wrong?" Audrey asked as she stuck her head into his cubicle. She looked at him over those silver-rimmed glasses, her lips pinched.

He straightened and coughed into his hand. "No, why?"

"You look like you're in agony." She gestured toward his laptop. "Is that piece giving you trouble?"

He glanced at the article on his screen. "Not at all. It's coming together great." Jesus, how could an article on the winter activities at the resort cause anyone grief? Not much happened here in Deerfield, nothing he considered newsworthy anyway, which was why he was currently covering the winter festivities and upcoming Valentine events at Stone Cliff. But looking at his article did give him an idea on where to start with Gracie.

Audrey gave a slow nod. "Good. I expect it on my desk at the end of next week."

As soon as Audrey left and he saw Gracie walk back to her cubicle, Nate turned his attention back to his laptop and messaged her privately.

Be ready at seven.

Where are we going?

The resort.

Why?

Wear something warm.

You know I can't ski.

Just trust me, okay?

He listened as she tapped on her keyboard and then came back with, *I really have no idea how skiing is going to help me with my comic strip.*

Do you always have to be doubtful?

You've seen my track record, right?

Oh yeah, he'd seen the kind of guys she went out with. Douche bags—every last one of them.

You just haven't been with the right guy, Gracie.

She stopped typing, and he could hear the wheels on her chair squeal. He looked around his ugly orange wall and saw her staring at her computer, like it had a live virus and she was about to catch it. When she started to turn his way, he pushed back in his seat so she couldn't see him watching her.

A long moment passed, then she finally wrote back. *Are you saying you're the right man?*

The right man to show you what love looks like, sure. He rubbed his palms together in anticipation, determined to open her eyes and show her firsthand how good they could be together. He knew he couldn't come right out and tell her.

Gracie had a cynical streak a mile wide, and he was going to have to navigate it carefully. No, he needed to take it slow and get her to open her eyes and see him as something more than her pizza and movie pal before he made a move.

Okay, I guess if anyone can, it's you. Considering you're in love every other week.

He stared at his computer a moment longer, surprised by her comment. Is that what she thought? Jesus, she had it all wrong. Sure, he dated—a lot—to keep his mind off the one girl he really wanted. When he did go out, he spent the majority of the night wishing he was with Gracie and that they could move from the friend zone and really give a relationship a shot.

He decided to change the subject. *What's for dinner?*

Your night to cook, remember?

Right. Let's eat at the lodge, then. You're on a deadline, and it will give us an earlier start.

Wow, you're going all out for me.

Nate frowned at the screen. *Was there sarcasm in that text?*

No way. I'm just thrilled you can help me. Honest!

It's what friends do.

Okay, meet you at the apartment later.

She signed off when Audrey stepped into her cubicle. For the rest of the day, Nate went over his article, made a couple phone calls, then left the office to talk to a few vacationers and compile some quotes on Stone Cliff.

Night fell early over the mountain town in the dead of winter, and instead of heading home, he made his way back to the office. Their apartment wasn't far from their work building, and normally, Gracie liked to walk home, but it was cold and the zipper on her jacket was broken.

He pulled open the front door just as she was exciting the building.

"What are you doing back?" she asked, dark lashes

blinking over those almost too big brown eyes as she lifted her chin to meet his glance.

Instead of answering, Nate looked over her navy blue pea coat, noting the way it was open at the neckline. He reached out and fussed with her zipper, which wouldn't budge past her breasts—lovely, ample breasts with taut nipples his tongue tingled to lick and tease. He coughed to hide his arousal.

"You need to get this fixed," he said.

"I know." She touched his forehead. "Are you getting sick? I heard you coughing earlier today, too."

"I'm fine," he lied. Hell, he wasn't fine, and it was getting harder and harder to be around her without touching her, kissing her, making her his once and for all. He tugged on the bottom of her jacket and gripped the zipper harder. "Damn thing," he grumbled and jiggled it, but his fingers slipped from the sliver of metal and brushed over the lush slopes of her breasts. He heard her suck in air, and when he glanced up, she had that pink tinge on her face again.

Looking for a distraction, he pulled off his scarf and wrapped it around her. He was about to tuck it into her coat but thought better of it. "Uh, you better do that." As she adjusted it and covered her exposed flesh, he frowned. "Where are your gloves?"

She rolled her eyes at him. "I'm twenty-three, you know. I can take care of myself."

"If you could take care of yourself, you'd be wearing gloves. You might come from out east where the winters aren't as cold, but you've been here a whole year, Gracie. You should know by now you need gloves." He pulled his off and shoved them over her hands. "Let's go," he said, gesturing toward his truck, which was still running.

"What about you?" she asked, the big gloves flapping as she waved them in front of her face.

"I'm good. The truck's warm. Besides, I grew up here. I'm used to the cold."

They both jumped into his truck, and a few minutes later, he pulled up to their apartment building and parked in his assigned spot. It wasn't much of a place, but it was all either of them could afford as they worked to pay down their university bills. He climbed from his seat and followed her inside.

"I'll grab a shower and be right over," he said as she started to unravel the scarf. "I think you should wear your black bomber tonight. It's warm and the zipper works."

"Yeah, good idea." She handed back his cold weather gear. "I'll put on some coffee."

"I won't be long."

"Okay, I'll leave the door unlocked." She unzipped her coat as the heat in the hall fell over them, and he glimpsed her hard nipples through that silk blouse as she nodded toward her place. "Just come over when you finish your shower."

He swallowed hard, because after glimpsing those lovely nubs, he was pretty confident he was going to come when he was *in* the shower. *Jesus.*

3

Grace started a pot of coffee and then hurried to the shower. She wasn't looking forward to hitting the slopes, but she was interested in seeing what Nate could teach her about love. And she was still holding out hope it involved him getting naked. A sound lodged in her throat. A half laugh, half groan. Honestly, who was she kidding? Nate didn't think of her that way.

She stripped off her work clothes and climbed into the hot spray, which felt glorious against her cold skin. She washed her hair and body, staying under the spray until the water turned cold.

She pulled back her curtain, and steam filled the room as she wrapped her towel around herself, knotting it at her breasts. Wondering if Nate was there yet, she padded down the hallway, not bothering to dress. He'd seen her in a towel numerous times, and it had never once pulled a reaction from him. Like she'd said, asexual friend.

"Hey," she said when she found him in the kitchen, doctoring their coffees. God, he looked good. Dressed in a fitted, blue pullover sweater that brought out the color in his eyes and a pair of jeans that hit all his spots just right, especially the one below his belt, he looked even sexier than ever. She liked him in his work wear, but she liked him out of it every bit as much.

He handed her the coffee and went back to stirring his, barely sparing her a glance.

She took a sip. "Mmmm, good." She leaned against the doorframe and watched him.

"You should get dressed," he said, staring into his mug like it held all the answers to the universe.

"Oh, what's the hurry? It's still early."

He coughed. "Yeah, but I'm starved," he said.

"Are you sure you're not getting sick?" She stepped up to him and once again put her hand on his forehead.

He breathed deep as her arm lingered in front of his nose, then puckered his mouth like he'd just taken a shot of Buckley's cough syrup or something equally distasteful.

"Vanilla," he murmured, almost under his breath.

She brought her arm to her nose and breathed in the scent of her new body wash. Was it that bad? "You don't like it?" she asked. "I thought I'd try something new."

"No, I like it." He coughed again. "I just think you should go get dressed." She turned to go, and he said, "Wear something warm."

"Fine," she said and made her way to her room. Honest to God, he was like a mother hen, always worried about her, probably because he was the oldest of four and always bailing his brothers out of trouble. Taking care of others just seemed to come natural to him. She pulled on her jeans and a big sweater. When she went back to find Nate, he was in her living room, shaking her Paris snow globe and watching the little white flakes inside fall over the Eiffel Tower.

"Still want to go?" he asked, holding the globe up and looking at her through it.

"Yeah," she said dreamily as he put it back on the bookshelf beside her small drafting table. "Someday."

He stepped toward her and met her in the hall. "What is it about Paris that you love so much?"

She shrugged. "It's the city of love. If only I had the money to fly there this week. I could meet someone, fall in love, and then all my comic strip troubles would be behind me." She gave a happy sigh. "Valentine's in Paris. How perfect would that be?" When a car outside honked and pulled her thoughts back, she shook her head. "Then again, what am I talking about? Love could hit me over the head and I wouldn't know it."

With a half-cocked grin on his face, he said, "For a smart girl, you're kind of dense like that."

"Hey," she said, whacking him, and even though he was right, and she was smart about a lot of things, when it came to love, she was clueless.

He feigned hurt, then grabbed her by the waist, pretending he was about to tackle her to the ground. He played football in university and liked to pull his moves on her. She'd just bet he'd learned all kinds of other moves at university. If only he'd pull some of *them* on her.

She grabbed his shoulders and yelled as he raced down the small hall. "Put me down."

He carried her to her closet and dropped her by the door. "Get your coat."

Grace pulled on her black parka as he shrugged in to his and tugged on his big, size twelve boots. She looked at his feet and couldn't help but think, *big in the shoes, big in the pants.* Not that she was ever going to find out.

"Hey, you ready?" he asked, dragging her thoughts back. She grabbed her hat and gloves as he pulled open her apartment door. They exited the building, and a frigid mountain breeze whipped over them. The sky was star-studded and so beautiful that she didn't mind the cold. If they were lucky enough, they might even see some northern lights tonight.

They jumped into his truck, and a few minutes later, they walked into the main lodge at Stone Cliff. The place was busy, ski vacationers milling about, talking excitedly about how many inches they were getting tonight. Since Grace wouldn't be getting any inches anytime soon—considering she hadn't been on a date in ages—she was less excited than the masses. Then again, *they* were talking about snow, and she was...well, she wasn't.

She waved to Jared, the concierge—a guy who knew everyone and everything and made things happen around the resort—and when she felt Nate's hand on the small of her back as he guided her through the throng, she leaned in closer to him.

Inside the restaurant, Jaelyn came to greet them. Gracie liked Jaelyn, and had seen her at the Cave quite a few times. The Cave was a place where locals and vacationers convened, drank beer around a bonfire, and hooked up at the end of the night.

Jaelyn cast Nate a huge smile, and when he smiled back, the pretty, tall blonde looked like she was about to shimmy out of her panties and hand them over him. "The perfect table just opened up," she said. "Follow me."

They trailed behind, and Grace couldn't help but look at the girl's perky ass. God, what Grace would do to have a tight backside like that. But no, she was gifted with a wide load that nearly registered on the Richter scale when she walked. At least she didn't beep when she backed up.

They followed Jaelyn through the dining room until she stopped at a table near the window overlooking the back courtyard, where several vacationers were taking advantage of the man-made ice rink. After taking their drink order, Jaelyn disappeared, giving them a moment with the menu.

"Can we do that instead of skiing," Grace asked, pointing to the skaters.

"Not instead of, but another time, for sure." When she frowned, Nate said, "Come on Gracie, I know you're going to love it when you get the hang of it."

She fiddled with her menu. "Then you don't know me at all."

He angled his head, his expression wounded. "Sure I do."

"Yeah?"

"Yeah.

"Okay, tell me what you know then."

His lips turned up at the corner. "Well, you're going to spend twenty minutes looking at the menu, debate over pasta and salmon, then decide on salmon because pasta sticks to your thighs and salmon doesn't. Then, when Jaelyn comes back, you'll order the pasta anyway and love it."

She folded her arms and glared at him.

He laughed. "How am I doing so far?"

Lifting her nose in the air she said, "You're completely wrong."

He shrugged like it was nothing. "Okay. And just for the record, there isn't a thing wrong with your thighs."

She made a face to show she didn't believe him then said, "Well fine. I know you, too. You'll look over the menu forever then order the burger." She rolled her eyes and dragged out her next words, "Because everything has to come on a bun."

"Yup, you're right." He closed his menu. "Burger it is."

Jaelyn brought their drinks, placing a white wine in front of Grace and a local beer on tap next to Nate, then grabbed her notepad. "All ready to order?" she asked, her gaze focused entirely on Nate.

He held his hand out to Grace. "What will you have, Gracie?" he asked.

"Pasta," she mumbled under her breath, twirling her wine

glass in her hands so she didn't have to see that sexy smirk on his face. After he ordered his burger and Jaelyn left, she turned things back to business.

"Okay, so I'm ready for my first lesson." She rested her forearms on the table and leaned toward him, wanting to keep their conversation private. "Teach me everything you know about love."

Nate's hands brushed up against hers as he looked around the busy restaurant. He gave a slight nod with his head. "See that couple over there?" Before she could turn, he whispered, "Look, but don't be conspicuous."

She casually angled her head to see some guy texting, paying zero attention to his girl as she sat there with a frown on her face. "Yeah, what about them?"

"What do you see?"

"Some jerk who's paying more attention to his phone than his date." She arched a brow and looked pointedly at Nate. "Don't tell me you see love in that."

He laughed. "No, you're right. The guy's a jerk. I'd never text when on a date."

"Any guy who is more interested in his phone then his date is definitely not the guy for me. I mean, for Kate."

"What about that couple?" he said, gesturing with his head.

"You mean the guy pouring wine for his wife?"

"Yeah. What do you see?"

"I see an accident waiting to happen."

He shook his head. "You're always looking for the worst case scenario. It's like you're programmed to find flaws."

"My job, remember?" She held her arms up in defeat. "What can I say, I write about dating foibles."

"Yeah, but now you have to start writing about love, so you have to start looking at things differently." He paused for a moment and stole another glance around the restaurant. "What about that couple? What do you see?"

She turned to see a guy shucking his girlfriend's oysters. "I see that someone is about to put an eye out."

This time, he laughed out loud, and his hand closed over hers. He gave a gentle squeeze that she felt all the way to her thighs. "What am I going to do with you?"

Oh, I can think of a few things...

"Tell me what you see then?" she asked, needing to get her mind back on her job.

"I see a guy who is kind and thoughtful. She's having a hard time shucking it, so he's helping her. I've seen my dad do that for my mom many times." He looked at the couple again and went quiet, contemplative. "I mean, she's capable, but he does it because he puts her needs first." He turned back to Grace. "That's why my dad always pumps mom's gas. She can do it, but he doesn't want her to get cold or dirty."

"So you're saying love is about kind gestures?"

He lifted his hands, and his eyes widened like she just had an epiphany. "Yes, and knowing what the other wants and needs."

"No guy has ever shucked my oyster." As soon as the words left her mouth, she cringed. "Wait, I think that might have come out wrong."

Nate laughed. "And that's because you've been going out with the wrong guys."

"I'm kind of a jerk magnet."

"Well yeah, the guys you date are jerks, but it's not your fault. You just don't know how to pick them or what to look for. But that's all going to change."

"You think?"

"Sure, you just need to start paying attention to the way the good guys treat their girls."

As she thought about that, Jaelyn came with their food. Grace grabbed her fork and dug in to her creamy pasta.

"Mmm, delicious," she said.

"I take it you're glad you went for the pasta?" he asked, a sexy grin on his mouth.

"Smart-ass," she returned, then nodded to his food. "How's the burger?"

"Good. I mean how can it not be?" He grinned. "It came on a bun."

They chatted quietly as they ate, and once they finished, Nate grabbed the dessert menu. Honest to God, Nate was always pushing her to eat sweets, even going so far as to stock his fridge with her favorite treats on movie night. He didn't care that she was plump, because he obviously never saw her as anything more than a buddy—to him, she was just one of the guys.

"What are you having?" he asked. "The chocolate mousse looks good."

She held her hands up, and even though Tess, the lodge's baker, made the best sweets, she said, "No way. I'm so full if I eat any dessert, I'll be rolling down the ski hill."

"Oh, and you think passing up dessert is going to change that outcome?" he teased playfully.

"Hey," she said, pinching her lips as she glared at him.

He grinned. "Don't worry, I won't let anything happen to you."

Jaelyn came with the bill, and they both reached for their wallets.

"I got it," he said.

Grace crinkled her nose. "We should split, it's not like this was a date."

Something strange moved over his face, a look she couldn't identify, then he said, "No I got it. Tonight was my night to cook, anyway."

She folded her arms and leaned back in her chair. "Okay, fine, but don't think paying for dinner is going to get you into my pants," she teased.

Nate put his hand to his mouth and coughed. Hard.

She eyed him carefully. He was either getting sick, or something else was going on with him.

4

"It's the bunny hill," Nate said. "There is nothing to be afraid of. Just do it exactly like I showed you, and you won't have any problems."

With her poles at her sides, Grace widened her legs, creating a wedge with her skis, and slowly started down the hill. Nate skied backward in front of her, giving instructions as she started picking up speed.

"Okay, widen the wedge," he said. "But keep your knees apart, like you have something between your thighs." A sound lodged in his throat, and he coughed to cover it as he envisioned himself between those long, luscious legs of hers, his mouth tasting, teasing, bringing her to orgasm over and over again.

"I think I got it," she said, pulling his thoughts back. They traveled down the hill a little farther, small kids whizzing past them, and her teeth flashed in a smile. "I guess this is kind of fun once you get the hang of it."

"See, I told you. You just needed the right person giving instructions, that's all."

Her wool hat started to slide forward, and she pushed it back. "You're a pretty good teacher."

"I've been giving lessons in the winter here for years. I even taught my brothers to ski." He watched her for a minute longer, and once she had the hang of it, he asked, "Okay, you ready to try a turn?" She nodded. "Remember what I said, tuck your right knee in, and we'll turn left. Watch." He flipped around and showed her, then started skiing backward again to guide her.

"Got it," she said, and he loved the excited smile on her face.

Nate kept a close eye on the way she put her weight on her left foot, her right knee turning in. Only problem was her hat fell over her eyes again, throwing her off. She pushed it up, but the movement tilted her off balance and she ended up crossing her skies.

He glanced at her face in time to see the panic in her eyes. "Oh, shit," he said, reaching out to help her.

"Nate," she yelled, but before he could grab her, she toppled right into him. Nate lost his balance, and they both went down, his body breaking her fall as their skis flipped off.

They landed with a *thud*, the momentum propelling them down the hill. He wrapped his arms around her, holding her tight to his body until they stopped sliding.

"Are you okay?" he asked, lifting his head to see her.

"Do I look okay?" she shot back, but he caught the quirk in her lips. She rolled her eyes, her mouth so close to his that all he had to do was lift an inch to kiss her if he wanted to. And yeah, he wanted to.

"I should have just had the damn dessert," she mumbled.

Nate laughed as her body pressed against his. An instructor stopped to see if they were okay, and after Nate assured him they were, he turned his attention back to Gracie, who was wiggling like she had an itch that needed to be scratched. Christ, if she didn't soon stop moving, she was going to realize just how much he liked having her on top of him. Just how much he wanted her. But he was pretty certain it was far too soon for that.

"We should probably get up," he said, but neither of them moved.

"Can't we just slide the rest of the way down like this?"

"Don't think so. And besides, you were enjoying it for a minute there."

She frowned and exhaled slowly. "Yeah. But this damn hat." She pulled at it. "I think you stretched it."

"Me?"

She crinkled her nose at him. "You borrowed it that time, remember? When you had to clear the snow off your car and couldn't find yours. I think you stretched it."

Taking offense, he shot back, "So you're saying I have a big head."

Her expression gave way to mock exasperation. "Well, you can't fight the evidence, Nate."

Damned if he didn't want to show her what else he had that was big, but since now was neither the time nor place, he rolled until she was under him.

"What are you doing?" she asked, sounding more breathless with each passing minute.

"Getting up."

"I don't want to get up," she said. "I told you I couldn't ski."

"You did fine."

"You consider me landing on top of you and the two of us barreling down the hill at supersonic speed fine?"

"It was hardly supersonic speed."

She pursed her lips. "You know, this scenario would be great for my article—what not to do on a skiing date."

He arched a brow. "But your article is on love, remember?"

She grumbled. "Did you have to remind me?"

She wiggled again, and he stiffened—everywhere.

"Shit," he mumbled.

"What?"

He coughed, but the jarring movement forced his hips forward, and his cock pressed hard against her pelvis. He quickly rolled off her and sat up. Taking deep breaths he worked to pull himself together.

"Nate?"

"Yeah?" he asked.

"I think we should get you home...to bed."

"What?" he asked, his head snapping around.

"You're doing an awful lot of coughing. I think you need to go to bed."

Well, she was right about two things. He was doing a lot of coughing, and he did need to go to bed. But neither one of them had anything to do with being sick.

5

After turning in her borrowed gear, and Nate stashing his in the locker he kept at the lodge, they left the resort and made their way through the parking lot. Fresh flakes began to fall as she climbed into the truck beside him. She cast him a sideways glance and noticed the tightening of his jaw as she reached out to blast the heat.

"Are you cold?" she asked.

"I'm not sick, Gracie," he said, his voice coming out a bit hoarse as the muscles in his jaw clenched.

She narrowed her eyes, and as the dashboard light cast shadows on his face, she looked him over carefully. "Then what is it?"

He rubbed his throat. "I just have this...tickle."

"Tickle? What kind of tickle."

"I don't know. The kind you get when something is...irritated, I guess."

"Can you scratch it?"

"No."

She leaned into him. "Maybe I can help. Show me where?"

He coughed into his fist, then gripped the wheel hard.

"Let's just talk about something else, okay? Like what movie we're going to watch when we get home."

She nodded and started listing off movies as he backed out of the parking space and headed down the hill toward Deerfield. As they passed the Cave, they could see a huge bonfire going. Flames licked the sky as music filled the air. Here in the mountain town, it didn't matter how cold or how warm it was, people could always be found partying at the Cave.

Once they agreed on a movie, she fussed with her hat as it slipped over her eyes and turned to him. "So tell me, what did skiing have to do with teaching me about love?"

"Nothing," he said as he carefully negotiated the truck down the slippery road.

"Nothing! Then why did we go?

He cast her a wry grin and gave a lazy roll of his shoulder. "Because I wanted to go skiing."

"Nate," she bit out and whacked him. "You're supposed to be helping me."

He laughed. "I'm kidding, I'm kidding. It had everything to do with helping you. By the end of the week, you'll see what I mean."

She eyed him skeptically. "I'm not so sure about that."

"You said you trusted me."

"I do."

He cast her a quick glance. "Then trust me."

He pulled up in front of their building and came around to her side. "Careful, it's slippery." His hand curled around her waist, and she leaned into him, loving the way he held her.

Once inside their building, he let her go. She pulled off her hat, and together, they climbed the two flights of stairs to their floor.

They reached her door, and with her body still chilled from the cold, she hugged herself and turned around. She was about to ask if he wanted to watch the movie at her place or his, but her head came back with a start when she found him standing there, staring at her.

"Nate?" she asked when she caught the way his pupils were dilating. "Are you okay?"

He walked in to her, backing her up. When she hit her door, he put his hands on either side of her head and leaned in, caging her against the door and his chest. Heavy, lidded eyes met hers, and it took all her effort to draw in air.

"Gracie..." he murmured.

Good God, he looked like he was in total agony. "Is the tickle getting worse?" she asked as his scent reached her nostrils and set off a storm inside her. "You sound so hoarse."

His nostrils flared as her body molded against him. "I told you, I'm fine."

"Okay," she said, still not convinced.

He sucked in a breath, and as he exhaled slowly, his glance moved to her mouth. "I need to ask you something."

"You know you can ask me anything."

"What would you do if I kissed you?"

Her heart stopped, because she certainly hadn't expected that. "Why...why would you kiss me? You could be contagious."

He closed his eyes for a moment, a pained expression on his face, and when he opened them again, his gaze dropped to her mouth, lingered a second, then moved back to her eyes. "I'm not contagious. I just want to show you what a kiss full of love feels like. You know, so your Kate will recognize it when she sees it."

She drew a quick breath to get her heart started again as she stared at him, trying to figure out what was really going on. Her mind raced, then she narrowed her eyes. "Wait, to kiss me with love would imply you love me, Nate. We both know—"

"That I'm in love every other weekend." He pressed closer, and his warm, familiar heat curled around her. "You said so yourself. So I would know what a kiss full of love feels like, right?" he explained.

She wet her bottom lip, and as a curl of heat licked over her thighs, she tried to remain calm. But holy hell, Nate was going to kiss her!

"Oh, right," she said, trying for casual, but her damn voice came out shakier than her hands. "Yeah, I suppose we should." Still holding her hat, she twisted it around in her hands so he wouldn't notice them trembling. "You know, for work purposes."

As soon as the words left her mouth, Nate dipped his head. The second his soft lips touched hers, her pulse took flight, sexual heat flooding her. Oh, God, he tasted so good—way better than a sweet vanilla latté, whipped cream, or any decadent dessert the lodge served up on a nightly basis.

Her body flushed hotly as he pressed against her. He deepened the kiss, the heat of his mouth pushing back the cold inside her. She moved against him, hungering for so much more from him. A noise sounded in his throat, something that reminded her of a growl, as his fingers fisted her hair.

His body crushed against hers, and her hat fell from her hands. With his kiss fueling her need for him, she wrapped her arms around his body, hating that his jacket prevented her from touching his bare skin, from feeling all his hardness beneath her fingers. His mouth pressed hungrily, his tongue moving against hers. His kiss evoked a myriad of sinful thoughts, like the two of them taking it inside, to her bedroom, specifically, where they could both strip down and take this love lesson to a whole new level.

"Jesus," he murmured into her mouth as his breathing changed, became harsher.

She moved against him, her body responding to the soft warmth in his voice as her hard nipples scraped against her sweater. Oh, Lord, what she'd do to feel them against his tongue.

"Gracie?"

"Yeah," she somehow managed to croak out.

"You doing okay?"

"I'm okay," she murmured, as her entire body came alive.

"Good."

His knee slipped between her hers, widening them as he sank deeper into the kiss. Her body went up in flames, because never, ever in her life had she been kissed like this. Jeez, if this was how couples in love kissed, then she sure as hell wanted to find her soul mate sooner rather than later.

Nate took off his gloves, his warm hands slipping under her bomber jacket to her waist. His thumbs brushed gently, sweeping over her skin in a way that had her senses exploding. Completely rattled, she ached to move against his knee, to quell the deep need between her legs. But cripes, she didn't want him to know what his kisses were doing to her—or how much she really wanted him in her bed. Nate was a player, a guy who'd reached out and touched more women than Hallmark—which, undoubtedly was why he was such a great kisser—and this was simply about teaching her, right?

Her thoughts dissolved as his breathing changed, becoming deeper, and when he adjusted his body, aligning his midriff with hers, his fingers climbed a little higher. Warm lips left hers and moved to the hollow of her throat, to that sensitive spot that ignited her blood to near boiling. She bit down on her lip to stifle a whimper, but there was nothing she could do to keep the fire inside her at bay.

"You taste so good," he murmured, the heat of his breath firing every nerve inside her. Her body grew slick, pressure brewing deep inside her, and she was almost certain she was ready to orgasm—just from having his mouth on her body.

The sound of footsteps racing up the stairs jostled her back to the present. "Nate," she said, pushing at him. She cursed silently, because dammit, she really did want to see if he could bring her to climax.

He stepped back and just stood there, staring at her. His nostrils flared and his chest heaved as he pulled in deep, gulping breaths. He shoved his hands through his hair. They came away shaking. Wow, she'd never seen him look so rattled, so intense before. Had that kiss affected him the same way it had her? The possibility weakened her already wobbly knees. She leaned against the door for support, otherwise, she was sure she was about to slide to the floor.

Someone cleared their throat, and they both turned.

Nate's second youngest brother, Sam, stood there. He took a small step back when they both zeroed in on him. "Ah, if I'm interrupting—"

"What are you doing here, Sam?" Nate asked, then turned his gaze back to Grace.

"Ummm..." Sam started, blue eyes that mirrored Nate's darting between the two of them, a bemused expression on his handsome face.

"Don't worry, you're not interrupting anything," Grace said quickly as she rummaged through her pockets, her heart hammering in her ears as she worked to cover up the kiss. "We just got back from skiing, and I was looking for my key. Nate was helping me."

Sam paused for a moment, then grinned. "Did you swallow it?"

"Sam," Nate warned.

"I mean the last time someone went searching in my mouth, I'm pretty certain it was for my tongue."

"Shut the hell up, little brother."

Sam turned to Nate, and still grinning, Sam scrubbed a gloved hand over the stubble on his face and said, "Whatever you say, big bro."

"Why are you here?" Nate asked.

"Oh, right. Mason just got in last night, and we're all heading to the cottage for a snowmobile run. You weren't at Grizzly's, so I thought I might find you here."

Nate cast her a questioning glance. She faked a yawn and said, "You should go, sounds like fun. Besides, you haven't seen Mason in a while." Grace had met his two other brothers, Sam and Josh, but Mason was away at university, and the two had yet to cross paths.

Nate drove his hands into his pockets and shifted himself. "I thought you wanted to watch a movie."

"I'm tired." She stretched her arms to prove her point. "I think I'll do a bit of work and then call it an early night. All that fresh air wore me out."

Nate stared at her for longer than was comfortable, then he asked, "You sure?"

"Positive." She shooed him away. "Go have some fun with your brothers."

With that non-negotiable piece of advice, he nodded and left with Sam. Grace let herself into her apartment, her body still feeling the effects of the kiss as she stripped off her winter clothes and walked to her small drafting table. She plunked herself down, her fingers going to lips that still tingled as she thought about the events of the night.

She grabbed her pencil and started doodling without giving it too much consideration. A while later, after she finished, she looked over her work, taking in the picture of the man shucking oysters for his girlfriend. At least it was a start. Upon closer inspection, it occurred to her that the man she'd drawn looked an awful lot like Nate. She dropped her pencil and jumped from her chair, her libido obviously still in an uproar from that unexpected turn of events at her door earlier.

Deciding to hit the bed early, she brushed her teeth and climbed between her flannel sheets. While she was tired, her mind went back to Nate, to that hot kiss. She ran her tongue over her bottom lip, and she could still taste the warm flavor of his mouth. His kiss had been so needy, so passionate, it almost made her think it was something he'd wanted to do for a long time. Her body warmed as she relived those few glorious seconds, and the needy juncture between her legs moistened, clamoring for attention. She bit her lips and wondered what would have happened if Sam hadn't interrupted them. Would they have made it to her bed, or his, so Nate could show her what sex full of love felt like? She gulped and shifted on her bed, willing her mind to shut down. Either that, or she was going to have to grab her trusty toy from her nightstand and finish what Nate had started.

She tossed restlessly, and even though he'd kissed her with hunger and heat and had her wondering if there was something more behind it, she decided it was best if she didn't read too much into it. She hated to get her hopes up, think there could be more between them, when in fact, it was just Nate being a friend and helping her. She fluffed her pillow and rolled to her side, and after pushing the kiss to the back of her mind, she finally fell into a fitful sleep.

Many hours later, bright rays of sunshine shone in through the crack in Grace's curtain, pulling her awake. She stretched out her limbs, her muscles sore from the fall yesterday, and then she wiped her eyes to glance at her clock. She kicked the blankets off and climbed from bed, her thoughts immediately going to Nate. Padding down her narrow hallway to her kitchen, she wondered what time Nate would head to the gym. If he was out late with his brothers, he might not want to go until later. Stopping in the hall mid-stride, she realized that she hadn't heard him come home last night. Their walls were paper-thin, and she always heard him on the stairs or letting himself in to his apartment.

Dressing quickly, Gracie grabbed a coffee and a slice of toast, then left her apartment. She stood outside Nate's door, listening for a moment before she tapped quietly. When he didn't answer, she darted down the stairs and caught the shuttle to the Stone Cliff, where she had a membership to the resort's facilities.

Making it just in time to join the early morning yoga class, she filled her water bottle and grabbed a mat. For the next hour, she put everything out of her mind and lost herself in the poses. When she finished, Erin Foster, one of the reporters for the Gazette, came bounding over to her.

"Hey, Grace," Erin said, her big blue eyes wide as she wiped perspiration from her forehead. She released the elastic holding back her long blond hair and let it flare over her narrow shoulders. "Want to grab a coffee?"

Grace nodded. "Sure." While the two didn't hang out often, she liked Erin, even though the girl was prone to gossip —maybe a little too much. That was probably just a reflection of her job, however. Erin was always looking for the next big scoop, just like Grace was always looking for the worst in a relationship. Now she had to write about love for the stupid Valentine issue. Her thoughts immediately went to Nate—his kisses. Her fingers automatically went to her lips. God, what she'd do to kiss him like that again.

"You okay?" Erin asked.

"Yeah, why?"

"You're so flushed."

"It's just hot in here," she said, swiping the towel over her face before stuffing it into her gym bag. "All set?" she asked.

Erin gathered her gear, and they left the studio and walked to the change rooms. After showering, they made their way to Coffee Stop, the small coffeehouse inside the resort's main building, and when the scent of freshly brewed java reached her nostrils, Grace breathed deeply.

Grace looked over the chalkboard menu on the back wall as she walked up to the counter. The Coffee Stop was a quaint place, filled with small tables, lounge chairs, and sofas in the middle of the room. Since it was still quiet around the lodge this time of the morning, they pretty much had the place to themselves. Grace ordered her favorite vanilla latté, along with a scone, and munched on it as she sat across from Erin at a table overlooking the ski hill.

"So," Erin began right away as she peeled the wrapper off her blueberry muffin. "What's going on with you and Nate anyway?"

Grace crinkled her nose. "Nothing. Why?"

"You two always hang out so much, and I never see him at Grizzly's anymore." Erin took a sip of her latte and casually added, "Although, he was there last night."

Grace's head came back with a start. "He was?" she asked, a little taken aback, even though she had no right to be. Sam had said they were headed to the cottage, not to Grizzly's, the local hangout and hook up. What they did and where they went after they left the apartment was their business, right? That amazing kiss didn't all of a sudden give her claim to him.

"Yeah, all four of the brothers were there." Shrewd eyes moved over Grace's face. "Why do you seem so surprised?"

"Oh, I'm not," Grace said, catching herself before she gave away too much. The last thing she wanted was to do or say something that could start rumors about the two of them and put a kink into Nate's social life. Yeah, God forbid she do that!

A dreamy look came over Erin's face. "Damn, those brothers are so hot. With all four in one room, I thought the fire alarms were going to go off." She exhaled slowly, then bit into her muffin. "They all look so much alike, don't they? Almost like quads."

"They're all only a year apart."

"Have you met Mason yet?"

"Not yet."

"I think he's the biggest player of them all." She swallowed and said, "When they left, they went to the Cave, and most of Grizzly's cleared out and followed them. I heard they were looking for Jared."

"Jared, as in, the hotel's concierge?"

"Yeah."

Curious, but trying not to show it, she asked, "Why were they looking for him?"

"I don't know. Maybe because he has his pulse on the action, and those four were looking for a little of that action, if you know what I mean." She wagged her eyebrows. "Not that I think they needed Jared for that."

"What do you mean?

"Come on, Grace. Those boys can have their pick of women, and it's no surprise that they'd left the Cave before I got there. It wouldn't take long for any one of the Wright brothers to hook up." She grinned. "Those Wright brothers are all kinds of right, aren't they?"

"I don't look at Nate that way," she said. "We're just friends."

As Erin gave her a dubious look, Grace sat back in her chair and fought an unwise pang of jealousy. Honestly, what Nate did on his own time was his business, not hers. She knew he had a healthy sex life, heck, she'd heard the giggles in the hallway when he brought a girl home. So why, all of a sudden, was it bothering her? She took a sip of her latte and swallowed hard, thinking perhaps that kiss had affected her more than she ever should have allowed.

6

Nate cast a sideways glance at Gracie as he drove to his folks' house for their weekly Sunday dinner, where they would sit around a long, oaken table with his three brothers, and mom and dad, and dine on a delicious, home-cooked meal.

Thinking about his brothers had his mind going back to Friday night when he'd caved under Sam's interrogation. As soon as they reached his truck, and Sam started in on him, he told him everything, admitting how crazy he was about his best friend and how he was using her comic strip as an opportunity to show her how much he cared. After spilling his guts, the two had grabbed their other brothers and went in search of Jared at the Cave. The five of them put a plan together—one, he hoped, would finally open her eyes.

As he glanced at Gracie now, it occurred to him that she'd been awfully quiet and a bit withdrawn since he knocked on her door earlier that day. He hadn't seen her or spent any time with her since that mind-blowing kiss Friday night. Saturday, after he'd returned from his overnight snowmobile trip with his brothers, she'd made herself scarce, insisting she had chores to do and her apartment to clean.

His gut knotted, and he couldn't help but worry if he'd kissed her too soon. But dammit, he was going out of his fucking mind, dying to finally feel those soft lips of hers pressed against his, to discover if she tasted as sweet as he knew she would. What he discovered was that she was way sweeter than he ever could have imagined. It was all he'd been able to think about the whole weekend. Christ, he nearly rammed his snowmobile into a tree because his mind had been so consumed with her and not on what he'd been doing. His brothers had a good time razzing him about that later in the night over a few beers.

"Hey," he said. She turned to him, and for a second, he thought he saw sadness in her big brown eyes before she blinked it away. She plastered on a smile, but he could tell it took effort. "Everything okay?" he asked.

"Yeah. Just worried about my job."

"Don't worry. By the end of the week, I'm sure you'll have it figured out." At least he hoped she would. He reached across the seat and gave her hand a squeeze. When his grip loosened, she jerked her hand away and placed it on the casserole dish she had balanced on her lap.

O-kay...

Shit, maybe he really should have bided his time and taken things slower. Of course, that *had* been his original plan, but when the opportunity to kiss her arose, he couldn't seem to help himself.

Sam had taken them by surprise, ending the moment before he could take her inside and show her how he really felt, which, when he thought about it, was probably for the best because while she quickly tried to cover up the kiss, all Nate wanted to do was scream it from the rooftops. Jesus, was it possible she'd never see him as anything more than a friend?

Then again, he remembered the way she'd become pliable

in his arms. They way her mouth had opened for him, kissing him back with hunger and heat. Oh yeah, and he couldn't forget the way she wrapped her arms around him and swayed against his knee when he'd pushed it between her legs. The movement was slight, but he felt it—felt the way her body had reached out to him, telling him she wanted something more.

So why, all of a sudden, was she giving him the cold shoulder?

He pulled his truck into the driveway and parked behind Mason's car. They both climbed from the truck, and he wrapped his hand around her waist to hold on to her as they walked up to the house.

His mother pulled open the door before they got there, a huge smile on her face. "Grace, come in," she said, taking the casserole dish from her. "You know you didn't have to bring anything."

"I wanted to," Grace said, her shoulders relaxing as she eased into conversation with his mother, Margaret. Nate knew Gracie's own mother had been distant growing up, and he loved how his mother had taken such a liking to Gracie, making her feel included. In fact, she treated her like the daughter she never had and always wanted. With four sons and a husband, Margaret needed Gracie every bit as much as Gracie needed her.

"Nice to see you too, mom," Nate said in mock exasperation.

"Oh, Nate, get over here." His mother's blue eyes twinkled as she wrapped her arms around him and gave him a hug.

"Momma's boy," his brother Mason called out from the living room, where his father and brothers were all sitting around watching football.

"Don't be jealous because she likes me best, baby brother," Nate shot back.

Margaret helped Gracie out of her coat then herded them both into the kitchen to deposit the casserole dish. The smell of turkey and stuffing reached his nose, and his stomach grumbled, ready to dive in now. He rubbed his gut. "Gracie, how come you never cook for me like this?" he teased.

"Because I'm not your mother," she shot back. "Mason's right, you are a momma's boy."

"Of course I'm right," Mason said, and when they all turned to him, Nate caught the way his gaze was raking over Gracie. "And you're definitely *not* his mother." Nate fisted his hands, hating the interest in his baby brother's eyes. Mason stood in the doorway, arms braced on the frame overhead as he zeroed in on Gracie. Without taking his eyes off her, he asked, "Aren't you going to introduce me to your *friend,* Nate?"

Nate cringed, noting the way he'd emphasized the word friend. Clearly, he was fucking with him, because after last night and their meeting with Jared, all three brothers knew where Nate stood with Gracie.

"Mason, this is Gracie. Gracie, this is Mason, but you should take my advice and stay away from him. He's trouble."

"Maybe I like a little trouble," she shot back, and Mason's grin widened.

"Now I like you even more." He pushed off the doorway and took her hand in his. "Nice to finally meet you, Gracie. I've heard so much about you." He kissed her hand, and Gracie giggled. She actually frigging giggled. Okay, he was going to kick Mason's ass after dinner, and he didn't care that his youngest sibling was the biggest and tallest of the four brothers and proudly wore the title of all-star wresting champion at university. Yeah, he loved the kid, but he was still going to kick his ass.

"What are you doing?" Nate asked, crossing his arms as he moved in closer to Gracie to lay claim.

Mason laughed. "Nothing, why?"

"Boys," his mother called out. "Play nice."

Mason continued to hold Gracie's hand, and ever the shit disturber that he was, he said, "I can see why she's the only girl you've ever brought home."

Nate gave his youngest brother the death glare as Sam came in from the living room. He grabbed Mason from behind, holding his arms behind his back.

"Cut it out, dude, she's not for you," Sam said. Then Sam looked at Nate. "One shot," he said as he dragged Mason into the living room where Nate tackled him to the floor.

Josh, his second oldest brother, and his father continued to watch TV while Sam stood over Mason and Nate as they rolled around and jabbed at each other. Josh and his father were such easy going guys and so laid back, they were practically vertical.

His mother called out for them to come to the table, just as Mason pinned his right shoulder down. Okay, so much for kicking his kid brother's ass. Honest to God, his brother was all kinds of contradictions. Tough as a fucking bear, but yet so talented and artistic. You wouldn't know it by looking at him, but he was an amazing musician, painter, and sculptor.

"Say uncle," Mason jeered, his legs pressing Nate's arms to the floor as he lightly slapped both sides of Nate's face, a move Nate had used on Mason many years ago, before Mason had grown into a gorilla of a guy.

"Mason," Nate bit out when he saw Gracie watching them, taking too much pleasure in the way his baby brother had him down for the count. "You're a dead man."

"Not from where I'm standing, he isn't." Gracie said.

Mason laughed. "That's right. Listen to Gracie. In fact, instead of saying uncle, why don't you tell her I'm the man? Yeah, tell her I'm the man, Nate, and that she should be with someone like me, not you. You know, a guy who has the optimal genetic traits a woman wants in her mate. Isn't that right, Gracie?"

Sure that his brother was going to start pounding his chest like Tarzan, Nate bucked, trying to knock him off. He'd be damned if he was going to tap out in front of Gracie.

"What kind of psycho-bullshit are they feeding you at university anyway?" Nate asked.

"Says the guy who is pinned to the floor."

Okay, enough was enough, and not only was that knee really starting to hurt his shoulder, this was downright embarrassing. Catching his brother by surprise, Nate twisted and flipped him over. Once he had Mason's shoulders pinned, he drove his knees into his chest to keep him down.

"Now, do you have something to say?" Nate asked, slapping his face playfully. Payback was such a bitch.

Mason simply gave him one of his charming grins and said, "Yeah, I really built up an appetite taking your sorry ass to the mat *first*, which really, when it comes down to it, makes me the winner." He looked into the kitchen. "Mom, can I sit by Gracie?"

"Fucker," Nate said, ready to strangle him. "And it's Grace, not Gracie," he said.

"That's not what you call her," he taunted.

"And it's not what I'm about to call you—"

"That's enough," his father, Gary said as he stood, stretched lazily, then shut off the TV. "Time to eat. Leave your little brother alone, Nate." He shook his head at the two and grinned. Nate smiled back at his father. There wasn't a man in town who loved his boys more than Gary Wright. "You're the oldest and the one who is supposed to be setting good examples." He shoved Nate with his knee, pushing him off Mason.

Nate jumped up. "But he started it," he said, reaching out to help Mason to his feet. Mason gave him a wink, and Nate ruffled his hair in return. Jesus, he missed the kid, but he seriously needed to lay off Gracie. Of course, Nate knew he was flirting with her just to razz him. That's what kid brothers did. Even though Mason was brilliant, as the youngest in the family, he was carefree, easy going, and fun-loving. Basically, he was the typical class clown and was always going out of his way to get under his oldest brother's skin. But when push came to shove, if anyone messed with a Wright brother, they messed with all four.

Mason darted into the kitchen and plunked himself down next to Gracie before Nate could get there, and over the meal, they talked about Gracie's hometown, which just happened to be where Mason was currently going to university. The two actually had a lot in common. Nate kept casting him glares, but no one seemed to notice as everyone was too busy eating and listening to Gracie and Mason laugh. His brother was a goddamn troublemaker, for sure, and if Nate didn't need his help this week, he'd break his damn neck.

Once dinner was over, Nate and Gracie helped his mother clean while the rest of the guys all fell back on the sofa to catch the rest of the game. His mother handed them their coats, and he caught the grin on Gracie's face as they walked back to the truck.

"What's so funny?" he asked as they climbed in.

"Nothing really. I was just thinking about something Mason said."

"Forget about him," Nate murmured under his breath, jealousy eating at his gut. He knew his brother was just being a smart-ass, but damned if he couldn't charm the bite off a snake. The last thing he wanted was for Gracie to fall for him.

"What?" Gracie asked.

"Nothing," he said and backed the truck from the driveway.

As he negotiated his vehicle through the snow-covered

road, Gracie laughed again and said, "Now I know what Erin was talking about."

"What do you mean?"

"She said she saw him last night at Grizzly's. She thought he was the biggest player of all of you."

"She said that?"

"Yeah." She chuckled again. "And she was right."

He clenched the wheel harder, wondering if Erin had told her he was there, too. Okay, so it was true, he had a reputation, and no doubt Gracie would think the brothers were all out on the prowl, when in fact, his reason for being there had everything to do with her. He was trying to get her to fall for him, and it would simply complicate his mission if she thought he was out with another girl.

"So, uh, did she say anything else?" he asked.

Grace turned in her seat and looked at him. He cast her a quick glance then focused back to the road.

"Like what?" she asked.

"I don't know," he said, staring ahead so she wouldn't see the concern on his face.

"She just said she thought Mason was a player."

"Do you think he is?"

She gave him a look that suggested he was dense. "Yeah!" she said. "He's a Wright brother, isn't he?"

He pulled into his parking spot, and they both got out. When he met her at the front of his truck, he asked, "So you're saying you think we're all players?"

"I don't think. I know."

He pulled the security door open, and she moved past him and headed to the stairs. As she climbed, he couldn't help but look at her sweet ass. Christ, he swore he was going to take it slow, especially after the way she'd acted after their last kiss, but damned if he didn't want to kiss his brother right out of her mind and make her forget she ever met him. Plus, she thought he was a player and he wanted to show her that she was the only girl he wanted to play with.

When they reached their floor, he grabbed her and spun her around to face him. Her eyes widened, and she exhaled quickly.

"Nate?" she asked. "What are you doing?"

His glance moved over her face. Jesus, she was so beautiful, and there was no denying that he needed her in his life, his arms, his bed. He rolled his tongue around a suddenly dry mouth and said, "I was thinking we should try that kiss again."

Her face tightened warily as his hands brushed with hers. "I..."

Her sweet breath fanned his face, and he stepped closer until her body was pressed against his. Desire twisted inside him, firing his blood. He brushed her hair from her face as his tension built. A pink tinge colored her cheeks as he put his mouth close to hers.

"What do you say, Gracie? Should we practice?"

A strange noise sounded in her throat, but when he wet his lips, he could see something in her give. In a voice that sounded slightly unstable, she said, "I suppose it wouldn't hurt."

Oh, she was definitely wrong about that, because it was going to hurt all right. In fact, it already hurt. He shifted as his cock throbbed against his zipper.

"So, that's a yes?"

"Yeah," she said, her voice a soft whisper as one hand went to his chest.

Nate closed his hand over hers, holding it against him as his other hand went to her chin to lift her mouth to his. Christ, he wanted her so much it was all he could do not to drag her to his place and take her for the rest of the night. But he knew it was too soon for that.

With her mouth poised open, he bent forward and brushed a soft kiss over her lips. He felt a tremble move through her, and his chest puffed. *Take that, baby brother!*

"Nate," she murmured, her fingers curling in his jacket.

Hearing his name on her lips, nearly sent him over the edge. Need fueling his blood, his mouth came down hard this time, claiming her, branding her with his heat, letting her know in no uncertain terms that he wanted her to be thinking of him and him only—today, tomorrow...forever.

She pressed against him and made a sexy bedroom noise as her mouth moved under his, kissing back with the same passion and urgency. Her hands moved to his hair, and she ran her fingers through it. His cock thickened, and he called on every ounce of strength to keep it together.

When he finally broke the kiss and pulled back, his heart thundered, because as he looked at her, he sensed he was getting to her and that she was actually beginning to see him as something other than a friend.

Halle-fucking-luiah!

She opened her mouth, closed it, and then tried again. "I...uh...."

Nate brushed his thumb over her kiss-swollen lips, put his mouth next to her ear, and whispered, "I'll see you in the morning, Gracie."

Grace sat at her desk and looked over the messages in her inbox. Too bad she couldn't focus on anything in front of her, compliments of a sleepless night. Cripes, Nate's kisses were definitely playing havoc with her hormones and her ability to get a good night's rest. She was either going to have to put a stop to them or make him finish what he started once and for all.

For a moment, she wondered if there really was more going on with him, if his kisses had more to do with wanting her than they did with helping her. As she considered that possibility, she opened the website for her favorite lingerie shop, considering what she'd wear if she ever found herself in bed with Nate. But as she looked at the models—the tall, lithe kind of girls he gravitated toward—reality hit like a cold snowball and smacked some sense back in to her.

"Hey sunshine," Nate said as he poked his head around the orange partition. "Audrey beckons."

"Yeah, I know. I'm coming." She quickly shut down the website and swiveled in her chair.

"Everything okay?" She looked at him and thought she

caught a hint of a grin before he wiped it away. "You look a little flushed," he said and stepped farther into her pod, his mere presence overwhelming the small space—and her.

She eyed him, taking in the gleam in his eyes. Was he messing with her? Did he kiss her and leave her wanting more on purpose? Did she dare ask?

"I'm fine," she answered, chickening out, too afraid to cause tension between them if this really was only about helping her. Trying for casual, she pushed from her chair and smoothed her hand over her pencil skirt.

"Are you sure?" He shrugged and drove his hands into his pockets. "You just seem a little...out of sorts."

She gestured with a quick nod to her computer. "Working on my strip."

His glance went from her to her computer, then back to her again. He came closer, close enough that she caught his familiar scent. She squeezed her thighs together.

"So you're telling me you figured it out?" he asked, his voice a bit deeper than moments ago. "Your Kate knows how to spot love when she sees it?"

"Not quite." She was about to push past him, but he moved with her, blocking her path before she could reach the hall, and when a warm shiver moved through her, she hoped he hadn't noticed. She jabbed him in the stomach. "Move it, or we'll be late."

"Gracie?" he said as he dipped his head, his mouth so damn close to hers she thought he was going to kiss her again.

"Yeah?" she asked, suddenly breathless, as her hand itched to go back to his stomach, to explore his hardness.

"Will you be my Valentine?"

"Your...Valentine?" She blinked twice and expected to find him smirking, but instead, he was staring at her without a hint of teasing on his face. "You want me to be your Valentine?" she asked again.

"Yeah, I do. Only thing is, we have to celebrate Thursday instead of Friday."

She angled her head and did a quick calculation of her days. "But Valentine's is Friday."

"I know, but that's the day your strip is due. So you have to have it all figured out Thursday night."

Her heart missed a beat as understanding dawned. This *was* about work, and he likely had a real date for Valentines. "Nate..." she began, although she didn't have a clue as to what she wanted to say.

"The latest you can turn your article in is three am Friday morning, before the paper goes to print, right?"

"Yeah, which means I should probably spend Thursday night working on it if I want to make my deadline."

"You'll make it."

"Nate—"

"Just trust me on this, Gracie." He moved aside and gave a wave of his hand. "Now come on before Audrey hands us our asses."

She stepped past him and strolled down the hall, feeling very self-conscious with him behind her. She stole a glance over her shoulder, and when he lifted his head, like he'd been staring at her ass, a sheepish look came over his face.

"What?" he asked.

He couldn't have been? Could he?

"Were you...?" She shook her head. "Nothing," she said and turned her attention to those seated in the boardroom, waiting for them. She walked inside and grabbed a chair. Nate dropped down next to her.

Audrey shut the door behind them, and all eyes turned to their boss when she sat. "I'd like everyone to meet Lexi Edmonds." Audrey waved her hand toward the pretty blonde seated across the table from Grace. Lexi gave everyone a smile and flipped her hair from her shoulders in a flirtatious way as her glance lingered on Nate. And why wouldn't she? The guy was smart, hot...single.

Grace turned to see him and caught the way he was smiling back at Lexi. When she felt a sharp stab of jealously, her insides clenched. Oh God, this was so not good. Nate had dated numerous women since she'd known him, and it had never bothered her before. Okay, that wasn't entirely true. It *had* bothered her, but now that she'd gotten a taste of him, felt his lips on hers, his body so close, she'd be lying if she said she didn't want him all to herself.

"Lexi comes to us from the Halifax Gazette and brings a lot of experience," Audrey went on to explain.

Oh, I just bet she does!

"Nate," Audrey said. "I'd like for you to show Lexi around, since you two will be working closely together."

"My pleasure," he said, his gaze going back to Lexi.

Sexy Lexi, who clearly wanted to be Nate's playmate...

"Grace?" Audrey said.

"Yeah." Grace lifted her eyes and took in the concern on her boss's face.

"Are you okay? You look a little pale."

"I...uh..." she coughed into her hand. "I think I'm coming down with a cold. I probably caught it from Nate."

Nate leaned in to her, his breath warm on her neck. "I told you, I'm not sick."

Grace coughed again.

"Why don't you go grab a drink?" Audrey said.

She pushed from the table, thankful for the reprieve, and went to the bathroom. She turned the water on and glanced at herself in the mirror. When she caught the look on her face, it took her back to yesterday, when she had dinner with Nate's family. She remembered the look on his face when she and Mason had joked and shared stories. As she thought about it, it occurred to her that the look on his face wasn't all that different from the one on hers right now. She put her hand on her stomach and thought about how she felt, how the idea of Nate and Lexi together—intimately—twisted her up inside. Her mind raced, then came to a resounding halt.

Holy hell! Had Nate been jealous of her and Mason?

Could he want her every bit as much as she wanted him, or were his hot kisses melting her brains cells and simply filling her with wishful thoughts?

8

"Where are we going?" Grace asked, unable to settle her jitteriness when Nate came to her door to pick her up for their pretend Valentine date.

"To the rink," he answered, looking past her shoulder and into her small living room. "You told me you wanted to skate, remember?"

"Oh," she said, surprised by this sudden turn of events as she twisted around to see what he was looking at. They'd spent every night together, dancing at Grizzly's, cooking meals together, watching movies, and meeting up with his buddies, Tyler Jackson and Jesse Parker, one an MMA fighter and the other a motocross racer who was here for spring break. During the week, Nate seemed to be going out of his way to keep her from the resort, now he looked like he couldn't wait to get her there. She had no idea what he was really up to, but easygoing Nate seemed a little anxious tonight, too. She turned back to him. "Are you okay?"

"Yeah, why?"

"You seem nervous about something."

He scrubbed his hand over his chin and gestured toward her closet. "Everything is fine. Grab your skates."

She paused, and while she loved to skate, she couldn't help but think she should stay home and work. "Nate, my article is due tonight, and I don't know what skating has to do with love."

"You will." He looked down, his brow furrowing. "At least, I hope you will," he said more to himself than her.

She wanted to ask what he meant by that, but he seemed a little apprehensive, so she grabbed her skates instead. Nate took them from her and tossed them over his shoulders.

"It's slippery out," he explained. "I don't want you to fall and stab yourself." He winked and added, "That would put a crimp in tonight's plans."

"Well, I wouldn't want to do anything, you know, like bleed out, and ruin your night," she said.

Nate laughed, and his mood seemed to lighten a bit. "Let's go."

They hopped into his truck, and he drove the short distance up the hill to Stone Cliff. He parked in front of the main lodge, then circled the truck to meet her. As they walked around the lodge, heading for the back courtyard to the man-made rink, he went eerily quiet, like he had something very serious on his mind.

She was about to ask him again if he was okay, but he stopped walking just before they rounded the corner. He grabbed her elbow and pulled her to him. Their bodies collided, and her breath caught as he dipped his head, his lips so close to hers.

"Gracie," he said, his voice a bit hesitant, uncertain.

"Yeah."

His gaze moved over her face. "I was serious when I asked you to be my Valentine."

Her heart did a little flip. Really? He was serious? Nate wanted her to be his Valentine!

"Okay," she said, forcing that one word out as her throat tightened.

He brushed his thumb over her cheek, the feather light caress causing a storm inside her. "I wanted to give you every-thing you wanted, to make this night really special for you."

"Okay," she said again, her mind racing wondering what he was talking about.

"I hope you like it," he said, giving her a little nudge.

She stared at him, confused. "Like what?"

Instead of answering, he walked her to the corner. She rounded it, and when she saw a huge ice sculpture in the shape of the Eiffel tower and lights all strung up around the rink, her heart squeezed inside her chest.

"Nate..." she whispered as he stepped up beside her. "Oh. My. God."

"Someday, we'll make it to Paris, Gracie," he said softly. "Since it couldn't be this week, I thought I'd bring Paris to you."

"It's beautiful," she choked out.

"You're beautiful."

She swallowed and turned to him. When she caught the intense way he was staring at her, her knees just about gave out. "When... How?"

"This week...and with a little help from my friends."

"Friends?" She wondered if one of those friends just happened to be Jared—everyone's go-to man when they needed something—and that's why he'd been looking for him the other night at the Cave. Maybe his late night visit to the local hangout had nothing at all to do with picking up girls. "What friends?" she asked.

"I know a guy who knows a guy, and then there's Mason," he said, nodding toward the gorgeous ice sculpture.

Her eyes widened. "Mason did that?"

"Yeah." His nostrils flared, and he moved closer until his body was pressed against hers in a totally possessive way. "But I don't want to talk about him."

She looked back at the sculpture and the significance of what he'd done—for her—washed over her like an avalanche. "It's...it's incredible. I can't believe you did this." She shook her head, incredulous. "You went all out."

He shrugged like it was nothing, but Gracie knew it was far from nothing. It was something. Something big.

"Hey, if it's worth doing, it's worth overdoing. Moderation is for pussies." He gave her a sexy grin and nudged her again. "Come on. We only have the rink to ourselves for one hour, then it opens to the public."

They pulled on their skates, and she followed him onto the ice. Small flakes started to fall, creating a cozy, romantic atmosphere. Their breath formed clouds in front of their faces as they skated circles around the rink, and as she looked at him, taking in his handsome features and the warm smile that spread across his face every time his gaze met hers, she could hardly believe he went through so much trouble for her.

"This is perfect," she said as her hat fell into her eyes.

Nate laughed, stopped in front of her, and pulled her hat up. "You're perfect, Gracie."

This time, he didn't ask if he could kiss her. Instead, his mouth dropped to hers, their cold lips warming as they opened for one other. His hand slid around her back, holding her tight against him. He kissed her mouth, her jaw, her neck, and every feeling she had for her neighbor, friend, co-worker came rushing to the surface, taking her breath with it.

Oh God, was this what love felt like? She'd always lusted after Nate. At least, she thought it was lust, but as he kissed her and held her in their make-believe Paris, she was beginning to believe what she'd felt for him all along had been so much more.

"Nate," she whispered. Everything about tonight, Nate, confused her and convinced her this was about more than her comic strip.

"Yeah."

Her heart missed a beat, but she knew she had to do this. She had to take a chance and find out if this thing between them was real, otherwise, she'd spend the rest of her life wondering what if and regretting not making a move. Sure, she ran the risk of losing a good friend, but the risk of not doing anything to make this relationship permanent because she was afraid to take a chance was far worse.

"I was thinking about Kate," she began.

"What about her?"

"Well," she started but stopped speaking when he inched back to see her.

"Well what?" he pressed.

She waved a hand around. "This is all so romantic and everything, but I have to write a happy ending for Kate."

He grinned, and like he was reading her innermost thoughts, asked, "And you can't write a happy ending for Kate if you've never experienced it yourself, right?"

"Right."

When she looked into his eyes, she caught the promise of something far more intimate than a night on the skating rink.

"I was thinking the same thing," he said.

"You were?"

"Yeah, I was. Come on." He led her to the bench, and they both removed their skates. He grabbed them and tossed them over his shoulder.

"Where are we going?" she asked.

"To give you everything you need so Kate can have her happy ending."

"You know Kate's not real, right?" she teased.

His mouth turned up at the corner. "Whatever you say, Gracie."

He led her inside the building instead of taking the walking path around it to the parking lot.

"But your truck is that way," she said, pointing to the front doors.

"Too far," he murmured, and that's when she noticed he was talking through clenched teeth, his body so taut it seemed to be taking a great deal of effort for him to keep his composure.

Her breath caught in her throat, and a shiver of anticipation tore through her as he walked up to the counter to book them in. She glanced around the bustling lobby, then turned to him when he grabbed her hand and led her to the closest elevator. When they reached the fourth floor and the doors pinged open, he grabbed her hand and practically dragged her off.

"This way," he said, his voice so hoarse she barely recognized it.

He found their room and slipped in the key card. When the little green light flashed, he pushed it open and looked at her.

Grace stood there for a moment, unable to breathe. "So this is happening. It's really happening," she whispered.

Nate paused and inched back, his expression dead serious. "You do want this, right?"

She took in the intent look on his face and knew there was nothing she wanted more. "Yes," she whispered, so breathless she could barely get that one word out.

"Then yes, it's happening," he said, the pleasure in his voice exciting her all the more. He grabbed her, pulled her inside, and locked the door behind them. He flicked the lights on, and she blinked against the brightness.

Silence fell over them as his lips found hers, and he gave her a gentle, almost loving kiss. One that held far more emotion than any other he'd given her. She resisted the urge to pinch herself, because if this was a dream, she sure as hell did not want to wake up.

"Gracie," he growled, his tongue tracing her bottom lip, a long, slow sweep filled with tenderness as he trailed the backs of his fingers down her cheek. Heat radiated from his hands, burning through her body. "Do you have any idea how good you taste?"

His hands went to her zipper, and he peeled her coat off, letting it fall to the floor. Then he quickly removed his winter wear and pulled her to him again, his hands roaming urgently over her curves. He explored her body, touching her all over, and all the while, she just stood there, her brain too shocked, too surprised by this turn of events to think with any sort of clarity.

He inched back, his gaze moving over her face. "Touch me back, Gracie. Please, touch me back."

A moan rose from her throat, and her hands went to his body. As soon as she touched him, palming his broad shoulders, his sculpted biceps, and the hard ridges of his stomach, he growled and backed her up.

"I need you out of these clothes, baby. I need you naked."

She gulped, suddenly very self conscious. The lights were still on and well...she didn't want him to see her naked.

"Can I have a minute?" she asked.

He gave her a confused looked, then took a distancing step back. She grabbed a throw blanket from the end of the bed and darted to the bathroom, leaving him standing there, raking his hands though his hair as he watched her duck into the bathroom.

Working to calm herself, she took off her clothes behind closed doors and wrapped herself in the blanket. She gave herself a quick glance in the mirror, then opened the bath-room door to find Nate standing exactly where she'd left him.

"What do you think you're doing?" he asked, his muscles flexing as he fisted and un-fisted his hands at his sides. His eyes were narrowed, his body tight. He looked like he was ready to blow a gasket or something.

Grace gulped. Cripes, she'd never seen that look on Nate before. "You said you wanted me naked," she croaked out.

"Yeah, that's right, and I wanted to be the one to strip you." He crooked his finger, and she walked toward him, trying not to stumble on shaky legs.

When she reached him, he fingered the blanket, his eyes never leaving hers. "What's this all about, Gracie?"

"I...nothing." She glanced at the light switch, and when she looked back at him, his features softened.

"Baby, I want to see you."

She made a move to get between the bed sheets, but he stopped her. "No. I want to see you. Right here. Right now. Drop the blanket."

"Nate..." God, what was she supposed to say? I don't want you to see all my jiggly parts? Talk about a mood breaker.

He shook his head, and as if he read her mind, he said, "Don't you get it? Your body is beautiful. I love everything about it."

"I'm not like—"

"Gracie," he said stopping her. "You're perfect." He shook his head. "Every time you come near me wrapped in nothing but a towel, it's all I can do not to grab you and take you. I've been going out of my damn mind. You have no idea how crazy your body makes me. How much I want you. I've been going fucking insane being so close to you and not being able to see you naked, to touch every inch of you, with my hands, my tongue."

Holy hell, was this really happening? Was he really saying

those things...to her? She looked at the blanket covering her curvaceous body and considered the model thin women he dated. "But I'm—"

"Overdressed. Now drop the blanket so I can see you."

Grace hesitated, but when she caught the heat in his eyes, the hard ridge pressing against his pants, a burst of confidence stole through her, and she dropped the blanket to stand before him completely bare.

A lusty growl ripped from his lungs as he stood there staring at her, his eyes full of want, lust...need. "You're perfect," he said, and as she looked at him, it occurred to her that no one had ever looked at her like that before or made her feel so sexy, so desirable.

"Nate," she said, her body shaking as his eyes drank their fill.

"Yeah, baby."

She pointed at him. "Now you're the one overdressed."

He grinned, his voice sounding a little unstable when he said, "Yeah, I am, aren't I?"

In seconds flat, he had his clothes off, and this time, it was Grace who stood there staring. She drew a shaky breath as her gaze traveled the long length of him. He was so incredibly beautiful with a fit, athletic body that was hard in all the right places. She swallowed against the dryness in her throat as her fingers itched to touch him.

"Come closer," he said, his voice thinning to a whisper.

She closed the distance, and his thumb brushed her cheek as his mouth found hers. He kissed her deeply, passionately, and in no time at all, she became lost in the sensations, lost in Nate.

He picked her up and laid her out on the bed, then crawled over her, her body fitting against his like it was made for him. A tremor ripped through her as his hardness pressed her against the mattress, her large breasts crushed beneath his chest. He trailed kisses around her jaw, her neck, the soft hollow in her throat.

"Vanilla," he licked his lips. "I fucking love vanilla." His mouth went lower and lower, until his lips were hovering over one nipple. "You have no idea how many nights I've dreamt about tasting you." His hot mouth closed over one hard bud, and she trembled from head to toe. "Oh, God, Gracie," he mumbled then went back to sucking, nibbling, licking.

"Nate," she cried out, raking her fingers through his hair to hold him to her as he flicked a nipple with the soft blade of his tongue. Desire seared her insides and her breath came in a rush. Everything inside her tingled as want settled deep between her thighs. She lifted her hips, but he seemed in no hurry to move downward, to the spot that craved him the most.

He inched to the side, and she could feel his hardness on her thigh as he paid homage to her other breast, one hand shaping her curves as he ran it over her nakedness. She moved against him, writhing with want, his slow seduction nearly killing her. She was used to wham-bam between the sheets, but Nate...well, he was taking his sweet time introducing himself to her body and learning all her likes.

His hand moved to her knees, and he urged her thighs apart. She widened for him, and as his fingers climbed higher and higher, a maelstrom of sensation erupted inside her. He shifted to position himself between her legs, and when she felt him gently ease open her lips with his fingers, a whimper escaped her.

He bent forward and licked her, one long, delicious swipe of his tongue that had her hips coming off the bed.

"Nate," she cried out and went up on her elbows to look at him.

He mumbled curses under his breath, then shot her a

glance and said, "Baby, you're the sweetest thing I've ever tasted."

A second later, he buried his face between her legs, his mouth settling possessively on her sex as his tongue circled her swollen clit. She could feel tension building in her body as he pushed a thick finger inside her.

"Jesus, you're so wet, baby."

Her blood raced as her body shuddered involuntarily when he reached the sensitive bundle of nerves inside that no man had ever found before. He brushed lightly, teasing her as he took her closer and closer to the edge.

He took his sweet time pleasuring her, like *he* was the one who couldn't get enough. His lusty moans of want and the way he seemed to be enjoying what he was doing helped shed the last of her inhibitions. She lifted her hips, moving against his face, and when his tongue finally made contact with her clit again, caressing her with the utmost expertise, shockwaves rocketed through her body.

Oh. My. God.

A hard shiver ignited every nerve ending as his fingers pumped deep, and she exhaled a breathy moan. She fell back onto the bed as pressure built up inside her. As he stayed between her legs, licking, sucking, taking her to places she'd never been before, her throat tightened with emotions. No man had ever put her needs first, taking his time to give her what she needed before he took for himself. In that moment, her whole world shifted, but she didn't have time to think about it, because Nate was applying more pressure with his tongue and doing the most delicious things with his fingers.

Grace gripped the sheets and reveled in the sensation. "So good," she cried out, a wheezing sound escaping her lips as her muscles began trembling. Blood pounded through her veins and she gasped, wanting to hang on, fighting to hang on, but knowing it was a losing battle. Her body wanted release and was determined to have it. She closed her eyes in sweet agony as heat licked over her flesh.

So much pleasure.

Nate must have felt the changes in her, because he punched up the pressure and asked, "You going to come for me, Gracie?"

"Yes," she cried out, her breathing growing shallow as she gave herself over to the magical things he was doing to her. She clenched around his fingers, drawing them in deeper as an orgasm tore through her. His groans mingled with her moans as he continued to lap at her, drawing out each pulse until she finally stopped spasming.

He climbed up her body, and when his eyes met hers, warm shivers of need moved through her. "Nate," she whispered, putting her hand on his cheek. He closed his hand over it, and his nostrils flared.

"Baby, I need to be inside you."

She nodded, and he hurried from the bed. He reached into his jeans, pulled out a condom, and quickly sheathed himself. A second later, he was back on top of her, and her body responded with a shudder.

He brushed her hair from her face. "Tonight, I'm going to take you like this, because I need to see you when you come. But tomorrow, just know that I'm going to take you fifty different ways. All the ways I've been lying in bed and dreaming of taking you for the last year."

She swallowed, and because her brain wasn't quite functioning correctly, all she managed to get out was, "Okay."

"Good." He reached between their bodies and rubbed his cock along the length of her crevice.

She moaned and closed her eyes.

"No," he said. "I want to see you."

The second her lids flicked open, he pushed inside, and she gasped as his fullness stretched her.

"Oh, my God," she cried out as he filled her completely.

Holding her gaze, he buried himself deep and stayed completely still, like he was savoring the moment. "Jesus, you feel good," he finally murmured.

She moved against him, needing more, and he began powering in to her, her body growing slicker with each hungry stroke. She rocked with him, welcoming each delicious thrust, and when she wrapped her legs around his back to hold him inside, it triggered a reaction in him. He pressed a possessive kiss to her mouth, and it touched something deep inside her—something that had never been touched before.

"Nate," she whispered, the pull between them so strong, so powerful, she knew there was no coming back from it. They'd always been close, but there was no denying that making love with Nate had changed everything between them, creating a deeper, more intimate bond. "Oh God, Nate."

He pushed her hair back and cupped the sides of her head, his breathing growing more erratic by the second. "I know, baby. I know."

She squeezed her legs around his back, and her nipples brushed against his hard body. He grabbed one of her legs and held it to his chest as he shifted positions, angling his body for deeper, harder thrusts.

"So good," she cried out, a new wave of tension building inside her as he pounded into her, like he couldn't get deep enough, like he was seeking more than just release.

"Baby?"

"Yeah?" She ran her nails over his shoulders, soft quakes beginning in her core.

His gaze swept over her face. "I'm afraid this is going to be fast," he said. "I've wanted you for so fucking long now, I can guarantee I'm not going to last long."

A thrill moved through her to know she did this to him.

"Take what you need, Nate." She cupped his face and rocked her hips, encouraging him to just let go. He began driving into her, seeking what his body craved.

As another orgasm built inside her, she grabbed his arms to hang on. When she found his muscles trembling, a surge of love rushed to her heart.

His groin pounded harder against hers, and when he slipped a hand between their bodies to caress her clit, she gave an erotic whimper and let go. Her liquid heat coated his cock, and as her sex muscles continued to clench around him, he growled, drove all the way inside, and stilled.

A second later, she felt him release, pulsing deep inside her. She hugged his sides with her thighs, holding him tight as he collapsed on top of her, his mouth going to her neck. He breathed heavy, his breath hot on her skin.

"You're mine, Gracie," he whispered into the hollow of her throat. "Mine."

She raked her hands through his damp hair, holding him to her as she worked to catch her breath. They stayed like that for a long time, then he broke the quiet.

"Gracie?"

"Yeah?

"You good?" he asked, a new tenderness in his voice as he lifted his head to see her.

"Yeah, I'm good."

"Okay," he said, and as she looked at him, took in the warmth in his eyes as they moved over her face, her heart swelled. Oh, God, she loved him so much.

Looking completely drained, he rolled beside her and pulled her in tight. "Let's rest for a few minutes, then I'll drive you back so you can get your comic strip down before your deadline."

"Okay." She snuggled in close, loving the way his arms held her so protectively. Even though she was exhausted from the amazing round of sex, she was too keyed up, too excited to sleep. As Nate fell asleep beside her, her mind raced, taking her back to the morning not so long ago when Nate volunteered to give her love lessons.

Thanks to him, she now knew that love looked like the guy across the hall. A guy who knew her better than she knew herself and would go above and beyond to help her and open her eyes to what was really between them. A guy who didn't just make her feel like a star in his sky, but instead made her feel like she was his whole world.

Love had been in front of her all this time, and she'd been too dense to see it—too insecure about herself to think that someone as great as Nate could love her in return. But over the course of the night, he'd helped her fight those insecurities, making her feel beautiful, desirable, wanted by him.

She considered his nervousness earlier in the night and couldn't help but smile. They were friends, best friends, and like her, Nate was probably afraid of doing something to jeopardize that friendship. He was right to worry, because no way could they go back to being friends after sex.

She stole a glance at the clock then slipped from the bed. Leaving him sleeping, she pulled on her clothes, tiptoed from the room, and made her way to the front entrance to grab a cab home.

9

Nate woke up and instantly reached for Gracie, but when he found her side of the bed cold, he jackknifed to a sitting position. Where the hell was she? He rubbed the sleep from his eyes and looked for a note, then checked his phone to see if she'd messaged him. Nothing.

Shit.

He pushed the blankets off and checked the time. That's when he realized she probably left through the night to go finish her comic strip. Dammit, she was supposed to wake him, not sneak off in the middle of the night without letting him know. As he thought about why she'd do that, a knot tightened his stomach. Could he have taken things too far and scared her off? But he'd felt her body beneath his, felt the way she'd opened for him, whispered his name when she came. There was no way she could deny the sex between them was perfect. Everything between them was perfect.

He grabbed his clothes from the floor and pulled them on. Just as he was about to open the door and go find her, someone knocked.

He opened it quickly to find Gracie standing there.

"Come here," he said, pulling her inside and closing the door behind her. He looked over her face. "Is everything okay?"

"I don't think so," she said.

His heart fell into his stomach. "Oh fuck. I fucked things up, didn't I?"

"Kind of."

"Jesus, Jesus, Jesus." He said and fisted his hair. "I'm so sorry. The last thing I ever wanted to do was jeopardize our friendship, Gracie."

She looked down. "Well, you certainly did that."

He cupped her chin and lifted until her eyes were locked on his. "What can I do to make it right? I don't want to lose you."

"We can't go back to being friends, Nate. We just can't."

"Fuck, Gracie. Don't say that." She pulled something out from under her arm and handed it to him. "What's this?" he asked.

"It's the Valentine issue. I thought you might want to see it. It's already gone to print."

He pulled opened the paper, and when he read her strip, his heart stopped beating. "Holy shit," he said as his throat tightened. After he read the words Kate Loves Nate, he lifted his gaze from the paper to find Gracie smiling at him.

"We can't ever go back to being just friends, because I never want to stop being your lover, Nate."

"Gracie," he said and pulled her to him. His mouth crashed down on hers, and he kissed her with lust, need, possession.

"So what do you think?" she asked, nodding toward the paper. "Did I nail it?"

He laughed as emotions pressed against his heart. "Yeah, a few times."

She laughed with him. "Just so you know," she said,

putting her hand on his chest and backing him up until his knees hit the bed. "I really am Kate."

"I know that. It's your middle name."

"And Kate really does love Nate," she said.

"Just like Nate loves Kate." He unzipped her jacket and pushed it from her shoulders. "He always has, you know. He was just too afraid of doing something to jeopardize the friendship."

"Well, he sure opened Kate's eyes last night when he did something...something big."

He cocked his head and gave her a wry grin. "Are you saying Nate's big?" When she laughed, he dropped a soft kiss onto her mouth. "I can't tell you how happy I am that Kate loves Nate."

He deepened the kiss, and she moaned. "Nate?" she asked, her voice a breathless whisper.

"Yeah, baby?"

"Why are we talking in third person?"

He laughed. "I have no idea. But I do know one thing."

"What's that?"

"Now that you've changed the direction of your comic, you're going to have to start gathering material if you want to fill a weekly column."

"What are you suggesting?"

"I'm suggesting we both call in sick and spend Valentine's Day together right here, in this bed. I mean, you did say you'd be my Valentine, right?"

She arched a brow. "What, no flowers and chocolate?"

He brushed his thumb over her mouth, and she leaned into him. "Are you craving something sweet, baby?"

She shook her head. "No. All I need is standing here right before me."

"And all I need is standing right before me, too." He

frowned and fingered the top button on her blouse. "There's only one problem, though."

Her eyes dimmed with desire as he pushed the button through the hole. "What's that?"

"Nate *is* craving something sweet, and your clothes are seriously in his way."

THE END

WRAPPED UP

 10

Carter Reed stuffed a stack of legal papers into a manila folder and tried to ignore the distress on Mayor Walker's face as he glared from the other side of the boardroom. Turning sideways, Carter snapped his briefcase shut with a little more force than necessary. At least the loud clicking sound gave him something other than Walker's anger to focus on.

"Carter—" Walker began, clearly refusing to let it go.

"The deal is done," Carter said. "You signed the final agreement yesterday. The contract is legal and binding."

"That was before I found out the buyer wanted to turn the church into a casino," the older man retaliated. Walker ran his hands through graying hair, and Carter studied the letters emblazed on his briefcase to avoid the concern in his opponent's dark eyes. It was *not* his concern. "There must be something you can do," Walker continued.

From his peripheral vision, Carter caught the mayor shifting his gaze. Carter didn't need to turn to know Walker was scanning the ski vacationers through the boardroom's glass walls as they bustled around the lobby at Stone Cliff resort. "This is a small community, Carter, and the resort caters to those wanting to get away from it all, not those wanting to gamble. We don't need that kind of trouble around these parts."

"What my client does with the property after purchasing it is not my business." Carter grabbed his wool coat from the rack near the door and picked up his suitcase. He'd check out of his room earlier that day and brought his bags to the meeting, wanting to put Stone Cliff Resort and the festive town of Deerfield in his rear view mirror, sooner rather than later. All the Christmas music, carolers, lights and parades were giving him a damn headache. "I'm just here to see that the legal work gets taken care of. Any problems you have from here on out will have to be taken up with the purchaser."

Mayor Walker rested his elbows on the table and pinched the bridge of his nose. "Come on. It's Christmas and that church is currently being used as a food bank. Right at this moment, the space is filled with volunteers preparing meals for those less fortunate. We can't just close up in the dead of the winter, especially since we've yet to find another location to set up a kitchen. When we started this deal, your client said he wouldn't be touching the property until spring and we would continue to use it."

"Things change." Carter wrapped his gray woolen scarf around his neck and pulled up his collar.

"Right, so then why can't the deal? Let's face it. If we had known things were going to go down—"

Carter held his hand up. "The law is the law, Mayor." He really didn't have time to keep rehashing the same argument. He was going to be late for his flight. "I don't make the rules, I just abide by them." Besides, even if Carter could reverse the sale—and there was no way he could—he wasn't going to blow his first job out of law school.

He'd worked his ass off to get where he was, and in fifteen years, he'd never asked anyone for anything. There were times he had even held down two jobs between classes. He was here to prove himself to the law firm that hired him straight out of university. The last thing he was about to do was go soft and dig for some loophole in the contract. Someday, he'd like to make partner at McMillian and Stratton. Failing to return east with a binding contract in hand because the town decided they didn't want a casino wasn't in his best interests. Carter had learned the hard way that survival and getting what he wanted meant he needed to play life like a game of chess—each move careful and calculated. Sure, the deal could very well hurt the town, but emotions played no part in this job. Or in life. Another lesson he'd learned the hard way.

Walker's dark eyes moved over Carter's face. His brow furrowed, and in an almost sad voice, he asked, "You're still young, Carter. Is this the guy you really want to be?"

This is the guy I have to be.

"Just doing my job," Carter countered.

"But it's Christmas..." Walker said, like that meant something to Carter.

It didn't. Not anymore anyway. There was a time he believed in the magic of Christmas. Believed that someday Santa would give a scared and lonely boy the only thing he'd always longed for when he was being tossed around from foster home to foster home. He could only assume Santa had permanently placed him on the naughty list because he never did get that family he'd wished for year after year. And really, can anyone blame a kid for acting up when the *real* kids in the home woke up to a tree full of gifts, and the puppy Carter had asked for was nowhere to be found?

He hardened himself as he thought back to that Christmas some fifteen years ago. He'd spent that whole month of December being extra good, making his bed, studying every night, and doing additional chores around the foster house. All he wanted was for the nice family he was temporary living with to keep him forever, to love him like he was one of their own, and, because everything had been going so well, for Santa to give him the puppy he'd dared to ask for.

Except that cold December morning had changed everything for him. That was the day he realized three things: no one gave a shit about the kid who'd been tossed away when he was a toddler; if he wanted something, he'd damn well have to get it on his own; and being nice never, ever paid off.

The mayor stood, and the sound of his chair scraping across the polished tile floor pulled Carter's thoughts back to the present. Walker crossed around the table and came up to Carter. The two stood nose to nose, and as he took in the fine lines bracketing the man's eyes and the worry pulling down his face, Carter squared his shoulders, expecting another round of backlash. What the man did instead confused Carter and hit like a sucker punch.

In a nurturing manner, Mayor Walker tightened the wool scarf around Carter's neck. "It's cold out there, son," he said. "And be careful on the roads, the forecast is calling for more snow, and the hills around here are pretty tricky for those who aren't used to them."

Disconcerted, Carter stood there for a moment longer, staring mutely at the man who had bundled him up with fatherly concern. What the hell? He sucked in air and took a distancing step back as something inside his chest tightened, making it almost difficult to breathe. As the boardroom walls seemed to close in on him, he turned to leave, needing— almost desperately—to get out of there, but when Mayor Walker said, "Merry Christmas, Carter," he stopped mid-stride and forced down the lump climbing into his throat.

Shifting his briefcase from one hand to the other and then cracking his knuckles to disguise his emotions, he took a quick moment to compose himself. He let his breath out slowly to expel the unwelcome things he was feeling and pulled the boardroom door open, ready to get out of the festive town that was making him...*feel.*

Without turning back, he said, "Yeah, you too."

Carter stepped into the lobby, where he was bombarded with Christmas music, scents of pine and gingerbread, and smiling staff all dressed as Santa's elves. He really needed to get out of this place and back to his one bedroom condo where he could forget that Christmas was just around the corner and lose himself in his work until the damn holidays were over.

He pushed through the front glass doors, and the bitter wind whipped around his face. Knowing he wasn't dressed for winter in this mountain town, he turned sideways to the hurricane force gusts and tracked across the snow covered ground to the parking lot. He drove his key into the salt and slush covered rental vehicle, then hopped in and blasted the heater. Winter might be damp and cold on the east coast, but it was nothing compared to the dry, frigid temperatures in the mountains.

Once the windows cleared, he began his drive down the slippery mountainside, following along the frozen lake. Numerous sirens sounded as he crawled through the town's center, and he shot a glance around. He slowed even more and drove around a mid-size car with a smashed in bumper. Negotiating the turns carefully, he passed another car that had slid into a lamp pole. As he crept through the town, the snow turned to ice pellets and pounded against his window, reducing his visibility.

By rights, he should have holed up for another night. Only a fool would be on these treacherous roads. He turned his wipers on higher and kept going. Call him an idiot, but he'd had enough of the town and their damn holiday spirit.

Peering through the streaks on his windshield, he caught a glimpse of a road sign just up ahead. Snow stuck to the edges and blurred the markings, but he was sure it was the connector road that took him to the highway. From there, it was just a short drive to the airport. Then he'd be free and clear of Deerfield forever.

He eased his vehicle onto the icy side road and drove a few miles, keeping an eye out for more signs. The farther in he went, the higher up the mountain he seemed to be climbing. Shit, he had to be going the wrong way.

He gripped the steering wheel harder, looking for a place to turn, but there wasn't a house or driveway to be found in the blinding storm. Deciding to do a U-turn right in the middle of the ice-packed road, he spun the steering wheel. His tires slid, and before he could get the vehicle under control, something ran in front of him. The car turned directions, and all he could see was a flash of blue before the back end of the vehicle hit something solid, sending his rental fishtailing toward the ditch.

"Jesus," he cursed. Once the car stopped sliding, he slammed it into Park and looked in his rearview mirror. With his heart still racing, he searched the ground and tried to see what he'd hit. Something moved, and he spotted a large white dog, a streak of red blood staining the freshly fallen snow.

Shit. Shit. Shit.

His stomach tightened and he swallowed as his mind raced to catch up. What the hell was a dog doing out here in the middle of nowhere? Seriously, with the way it had darted in front of him, it was almost like it was asking to get hit.

Carter looked out his ice-crusted window, but since he hadn't passed a house in miles, it wasn't like he could knock on a door and find an owner. No, helping the animal meant taking it back to town and searching for a vet—none of which he had time for. He pounded on the steering wheel and considered his next move. What the fuck was he supposed to do now? He looked in the mirror again. The dog lift its head and meet his gaze, and he felt a small measure of relief. At least he hadn't killed it.

He waited a moment longer and tapped his thumb on his leg. "Come on, boy. Get up, get up," he murmured.

As the animal continued to lie there, Carter looked at the ditch and how close he'd come to sliding into it. Not sure if the vehicle was stuck after spinning out, he put it into gear and held his breath. With the way his luck was running, he'd likely be stranded in this Podunk town until spring thaw. He pressed on the gas and let loose a sigh of relief when the tires gripped the slippery ground. The car slowly inched forward, snow crunching beneath the rubber treads. A spray of slush spit backward as he picked up momentum. If he hit the brakes now, he was likely to go off the road, which wouldn't do him or the dog any good. Maybe when he got out to the main road, he could call the police although with the amount of sirens he'd heard earlier, they were probably pretty tied up with all the fender benders.

He looked at the dashboard clock. If he kept going, he could still make it to the airport in time, and getting back home was more important than anything, right? Decision made, he looked over his shoulder, but when he caught site of the dog, he felt something inside him give.

"Fuck," he cursed and slammed the car into Park. He pulled on handle to get out, and a strong breeze snatched the door from his hands, nearly tearing it clean off its hinges.

"Great," he mumbled. At least he'd bought the extra insurance. He jumped from the driver's seat, and the cold air stole the breath from his lungs as he tried to close the door against the strong winds. He put his weight in to it, but the metal latch was bent and twisted, and no matter how hard he tried, it still wouldn't catch. After another round of curses, he left the door banging in the wind and turned toward the dog. Giving up on the idea that he was going to make his flight, he grabbed a blanket from the trunk and cautiously walked toward the animal. His leather dress shoes sank into the snow as he trudged forward.

"Hey boy," he said as he approached, not wanting to frighten the guy any more than it was. "It's okay, boy."

The dog lifted its head and when Carter stared into the creature's blue eyes—the bluest eyes he'd ever seen—his head came back with a start. What kind of dog was this?

"Hey," he whispered, going down onto his knees when the dog whined. He draped the blanket over it and bent forward. The dog licked his face, a big, sloppy kiss across the mouth. Carter winced and pulled back.

"Come on, buddy. You're not my type."

The dog started panting as Carter wiped the slop off his face with the back of his sleeve. "And a breath mint wouldn't kill ya, either." The hound lifted his head and tried to lick him again. "Oh, no you don't." Despite the situation, Carter laughed, and as the dog looked up at him with those big, soulful eyes, he wondered how he ever could have thought about just leaving him.

"Is this the guy you really want to be?"

Dammit, why the hell was he letting Walker into his head, letting his words get to him? Who he was and what he did was none of Walkers business, and he'd long ago given up caring what people thought of him.

As something tugged at his emotions, he pushed that from his mind and ran his hand over the dog's matted, white fur. "Easy boy. I'm going to get you to the vet." When the animal relaxed against his touch, he picked it up, ready to carry him to his car, but the sound of a vehicle coming to a halt behind him had him turning. He felt a measure of relief when he saw a huge SUV, which was far better equipped for these icy roads than his rental. Perhaps the guy driving could give the dog a lift to town.

The door opened, and while he expected to see some big lumberjack climb out, the petite girl hopping to the ground in a pair of arctic boots that came to her knees and a coat that met them from the top side had him doing a double take.

"You okay?" she asked, her big brown eyes pretty much all he could see through the fur lined hood covering ninety percent of her face.

"I need to get this dog to the vet," he shouted over the driving wind. "I hit him with the car."

She glanced at his driver's side door banging in the wind, then took another step closer. Her eyes widened with something that looked like fascination as she zeroed in on the bundle in his arms.

"What?" he asked, her reaction confusing him.

"Uh, do you have any idea what you're holding?"

"A dog," he said. What the hell was she getting at? Christ, he might not be from the country where dogs obviously ran free, but he knew a dog when he saw one. And he might be an idiot for driving in this weather, but he wasn't a moron.

She held a gloved hand toward the bundle in his arms. "Hate to break it to you, City, but that's no dog."

The fear in City's eyes had Josie grinning, but she knew he had nothing to worry about. In fact, the mystical creature he was cradling excited Josie beyond words.

"If it's not a dog then what is..." His words fell off as understanding moved over his face. "Oh, shit."

"Come on," she said. "Put him in the back seat of my truck. Your car isn't going anywhere anytime soon."

"Are you sure?" he asked, those light blue eyes of his looking over the animal cautiously, like it was the big bad wolf and he was little red.

"Positive. Now hurry before you freeze to death." Josie's glance left his handsome face and traveled downward to take in his wool coat, dress pants, and leather shoes. "You're not dressed properly to be outside for any length of time, so you'd better hurry."

She opened the back door, and City gently laid the wolf on the seat. He fixed the blanket around the animal's powerful, streamlined body, and once he was secure, Josie climbed behind the wheel. City slid into the passenger seat beside her and rubbed his hands together. Seeing how cold he was, Josie jacked up the heat, put the SUV into gear, and headed up the mountain.

"Wait, where are you going?" He jerked his thumb toward the back seat. "I need to get him to the vet."

She peered through the streaked windshield, struggling to find her way in the white wash. "I can't go back."

"Then at least take me back to my car so I can."

"I'm afraid I can't do that, either."

He looked at the road behind them. "Why not?"

"A tree blew down behind me and blocked the road. We'll have to wait for a crew to clear it, and who knows how long that will be."

"You've got to be kidding me."

"I'd never kid about something like that," she said.

He looked at the animal again. "What about the wolf? He needs attention."

"I can take care of him."

His eyes narrowed, and she didn't miss the way he looked her over, not that he could actually see her behind all her winter wear. "Are you a vet?"

"No, a biologist. I've been studying wolf behavior for the last year." She shot him a quick glance. "Working on my thesis."

He went quiet and she could almost hear the wheels spinning. "Does that make you qualified to bandage him up?"

"No, but what other choice do we have? I'm sure, between the two of us, we can help him." She gave him a smile. "What are you doing out here in the middle of a snow storm, anyway? These mountains are no place for a city boy."

"Which is why I was trying to get to the airport."

"You know you're going the wrong way, right?"

"Yeah, I got lost and was about to turn around when that dog—or wolf, I guess—came out of nowhere."

Josie turned the wipers on faster and leaned toward the windshield. "It didn't come out of nowhere," she stated.

"Yeah, it did." He glanced into the back seat. "I blinked and he was just there in the road."

She drove higher up the mountain, then turned into a small driveway, the snow on the ground nicely packed down from her vehicle's big tires. "You can stay with me until the road is cleared. It's only a one bedroom, but the sofa is pretty comfy."

He gave her a look that suggested she was insane. "You're just going to let a stranger into your place."

She turned her head. Their glances met and she asked, "Are you dangerous, City?"

"No."

"Okay then."

His head came back, incredulous. "You're just going to take my word on it?"

"Not really." She pointed to the back seat. "I'm taking his."

"Uh, what?"

This time, his look not only suggested that she was crazy, but there was a good chance she'd just escaped from some asylum. She laughed and went on to explain. "I suppose I should probably tell you about the legend of the white wolf."

"There's a legend?"

"Yeah, and while I've always heard about the white wolf with the blue eyes that roamed these mountains, all this time, I'd yet to see him for myself. I'm pretty excited about it, actually." She put the SUV into Park and waved her glove at him. "The wolf is a symbol of luck."

"Luck? How lucky can he be?" He glanced at the semiconscious animal. "I damn near killed him."

"I don't think so. He got hit because he wanted to get hit.

He sensed you needed something and was testing you to see if you were worthy of his magic."

His eyes narrowed, and she tried not to laugh at the horrified look he was giving her. Right about now, he was probably thinking *he* should be the one afraid to be alone with *her*, instead of the other way around.

"So do you spend a lot of time alone in these woods?" he asked.

Unable to hold it in any longer, she chuckled. "Yes, but that has nothing to do what I'm telling you. I grew up here and have heard stories about the white wolf since I was a kid."

"Stories are told for entertainment. That doesn't mean there is a legend, or magic."

"Ah, the non-believer. Doesn't surprise me, really. Being a city boy and all." She shrugged. "Still, there is a legend. Do you want to hear it?"

"Something tells me even if I say no, you're going to tell me anyway."

"Right." She twisted in her seat to see him better. "Okay, so the white wolf is a legendary spiritual and shows itself as a wolf to those who need him. And now, because you stopped to help him, he'll stay with you until you have everything you need."

A noise sounded in his throat, a half laugh, half moan. "I hate to break it to you, but if that was the case, then I'd be about to board my plane."

"Is that what you want?"

"Yes."

Her mouth turned up at the corner. "Well, I never said he'd give you what you *want*, City. I said he'd give you what you *need*."

"Is this some kind of joke?" He looked around like he was searching for a hidden camera. "I feel like Scrooge in a holiday special, about to get a visit from the three ghosts of Christmas."

She gave another shrug. "I don't know what to tell you, City, other than you might be stuck here for a few days."

"The name's Carter," he said.

"I know." Turning from him, Josie opened her door and jumped from the truck. "Let's get him inside."

City climbed out, and the second he opened the back door, the wolf sat up, jumped from the back seat, and darted in to the woods.

"What the hell?"

Josie ran around to his side of the truck and clapped excitedly as she watched the animal run off, his beautiful, powerful body completely healed as it effortlessly negotiated the mountainous trail. "He's okay," she said. "I knew he would be."

City scrubbed his chin. "I hit him. I saw the blood. How did he…"

"I told you, the white wolf is magical. Now come on. Let's get inside and get you out of those clothes."

Carter stepped into the small cabin and was instantly assaulted with two wet noses in his crotch. Well, wasn't his day just going from bad to worse? He jerked backward, but there was no escaping the curious hounds.

"Meet Sasha and Bear," she said, ruffling the heads on her two big dogs.

"You have dogs."

"Way to state the obvious," she teased. Then she looked at him. "Wait, you don't like dogs?"

"Something like that." It wasn't that he didn't like them. Not really. It was just that he'd given up on wanting one. He'd long ago decided that he didn't need a dog and a dog didn't need him. In fact, he didn't need anybody. Not anymore, anyway. He pulled his cell phone from his pocket and checked for a signal.

"It might be hard to get a signal. Too many mountains." She grabbed her dogs by their collars and put them outside. She closed the door behind them and kicked off her boots, leaving them in the middle of the floor.

Giving up on his phone, he stuffed it back into his coat pocket. "How do you communicate?"

Whipping off her gloves and tossing them onto a small side table, she pointed to a landline. "The old fashion way."

"Do you even have internet?"

"Of course. This is Stone Cliff, not the stone ages." She pointed to her laptop that was currently plugged into the wall. "All the cottages are equipped with internet."

She shrugged out of her jacket, tugged off her hat, and tossed them onto the back of the sofa. As she flung things haphazardly, Carter flinched and resisted the urge to grab her coat and hang it up properly.

She turned to him, and the second he saw her pretty face, along with a petite body all wrapped up in tight jeans and a soft white sweater that showcased her curves, he almost forgot how to breathe. Jesus, she was cute, in a wholesome, girl-next-door kind of way. Blonde hair in a messy little pixie cut that most girls couldn't pull off made her looks all that much more adorable. She blinked those big brown eyes at him, and in that instant, his thoughts shifted. Wouldn't it be nice to hole up in a cabin in the middle of nowhere with a sweet thing like her. There were a lot of ways could do to pass the time.

"You hungry?"

Carter sucked in a breath to kick-start his brain and caught the smell of gingerbread and everything Christmas. He stole a glance around the small cabin, taking in the decorations, the massive tree, and all the twinkling lights on the windows. Not only was the place the epitome of Christmas, she even had a goddamn fire going in the wood stove. Seriously? Had he just stepped right into a holiday special?

He shot a glance around to look for a hidden camera. Of all the girls in all the world to come to his rescue, it had to be one who loved Christmas as much as he hated it. She pushed past him and flicked on the radio. When holiday music reached his ears, he turned toward the door, because no way in hell was he staying in this cottage—which might as well have been Santa's village in the north pole—for one more second. He wanted to forget about the holidays, and being here with a girl who clearly loved them just wasn't going to work for him.

"I've got a ton of food," she said as she pulled open her fridge. "I guess it's a good thing I found you on the road. Now I have someone to share it with."

He looked into her stocked fridge. Why the hell did she have so much food? Perhaps she didn't live alone. He checked her ring finger to find it empty, but that didn't mean she didn't have a guy who couldn't make it home. Damn, if he had a sweet thing like her waiting, he'd brave the storm barefoot. Wait, what? Hadn't he just decided he needed to get the hell out of there?

"Listen, I really need to get back to my car," he said.

She pulled a big turkey from the fridge and placed it beside a tray full of sugar cookies on her counter. His stomach took that moment to grumble, a reminder that it was late afternoon and he hadn't eaten since breakfast.

"What's the hurry?" She grabbed a knife and began carving thick pieces from the breast, laying them out on a plate.

The dogs barked at the door, and she waved her knife toward it. "Would you mind letting them in?" She smiled. "They probably smell the turkey."

"You feed your dogs turkey?"

She nodded. "Sure."

Carter pulled open the door, and the wet dogs barreled past him, shaking snow all over the wood floor. They skidded to a halt near...come to think of it, he didn't even know her name.

"What's your name?"

"Josie," she said, filling the dog bowls with meat.

Josie. It was cute, like her.

"I'm Carter," he said, introducing himself again.

Her dogs stared at her, and she gave the command for them to eat. They raced to their bowls. "I know who you are."

He eyed her. "How is it you know me again?"

Swaying to the Christmas tune, she grabbed a loaf of bread and a bottle of cranberry sauce. "Everyone in town knows who you are and why you're here."

Ah yes, he should have known. Another local who hated him after finding out about his client's plans. "Then why are you being so nice to me?"

"It's Christmas," she said, like that explained everything. Damned if she didn't have the same attitude as Mayor Walker.

As she spread cranberry sauce on the slices of bread and loaded them with turkey, he glanced out the frosty window, but the snow was coming down so hard he could barely see her truck.

"You can come in, you know."

He turned back to find Josie smiling at him. "What?"

"You're still standing at the door."

"That's because I'm not staying."

"No?" she asked.

He did a quick calculation and estimated the time it would take for him to reach his car by foot. "I'm going to go back to my car and grab my bag. If I walk to the main road, maybe someone will come by and I can catch a lift to the airport."

"Okay," she said. "Suit yourself. You already missed your plane, so you might as well have something to eat and let me hook you up with some warmer clothes. You're going to burn a lot of energy trudging from your car to the main road."

"Yeah, okay."

She disappeared behind one of the closed doors and came back with an armload of clothes. "I think these will fit." She pointed to the one other door. "Bathroom is in there."

She watched, almost amused, as he tugged off his heavy, wet wool coat and hung it on the empty coat rack by the door. He removed his soggy shoes, placed them on the mat, and then, unable to help himself, grabbed her boots and set them beside his.

He took the armload of clothes from her as her dogs finished eating and cantered off to their beds in front of the fire. "You don't think whoever owns these will mind?" Yeah, he was fishing for information, not because he was curious about her status, but because he wanted to know if she had a boyfriend who was going to show up and kick his ass for being there alone with her.

She shook her head and said, "No, I don't think so."

He tossed the clothes over his shoulder and made his way to the bathroom. After undressing, he tugged on the jeans, warm socks, and sweater. He folded his clothes carefully and left the bathroom to find Josie talking quietly on the phone. She hung up when she heard him and went back to setting the table.

Carter put his wet clothes on the mat beside the door and held out his arms. "It's a good thing your boyfriend is the same size as me."

She turned to him. "I..." her words fell off as her glance left his face and traveled downward. Her gaze lingered for a moment on his stomach, then dropped to the vicinity around his belt. Her eyes widened.

"Oh," she said.

He checked his zipper. "What?"

She went back to laying out napkins. "Nothing."

Wait! Was she checking him out?

Hell yeah, she was. That was interest in her eyes. Carter moved toward her, his stomach grumbling louder as he looked over the table and the tray of finger sandwiches she made for them. He couldn't help but grin when she filled the two tall glasses beside their plates.

"Milk?"

She topped up his glass. "A growing boy needs milk."

He laughed. Was she for real? Honest to God, where he came from, he'd have to search high and low for someone as innocent and wholesome as her, and he was still pretty sure he'd come up empty-handed.

"I'm twenty four. I stopped growing years ago," he said.

She pulled out her chair and sat. "We'll see."

Even though he had no idea what she was talking about, he lowered himself into the seat across from her and took a big drink. He couldn't remember the last time he'd had a glass of milk or home cooked turkey on whole grain bread. These days, he mostly ran on coffee and take out.

"Help yourself." She waved her hand over the tray of sandwiches, then placed one on the plate in front of her. "There's plenty more where these came from."

Carter grabbed one and took a big bite, nearly eating the whole thing at once. Lord, that had to be the best thing he'd ever tasted. He chewed, swallowed, then shoved the rest into his mouth, chasing it with a swig of milk.

"Good," he said, reaching for another.

"Thanks." A wide smile split her lips, and he damn near choked on his food. She was so sweet and...sexy.

Even though they were opposite in almost every way, he was a guy, and guys thought about sex. A lot. Well, at least he did. She licked cranberry sauce from her lips and he stifled a groan. Damn, she had the nicest mouth. He didn't know much about her, but he could only imagine she'd taste as sweet as the cookies on her counter. For a brief moment, he thought about kissing her to find out.

But he quickly squashed that thought. A sweet girl like her probably took her relationships seriously and would likely want more than he could give. All he could offer her was a quick, hot lay, and nothing more. Logic dictated it was time to stop thinking about her sexually. And, of course, he couldn't forget about the boyfriend who was still out there.

She leaned forward to grab another finger sandwich. He caught a flash of her creamy white skin and his damn cock thickened. O-kay. So apparently he *was* a growing boy, after all. Okay, a hot roll in the sack would be nice, but since every move he made was careful and calculated, he needed to get his shit together. Sleeping with a sweet thing like her was not in his own best interests, for numerous reasons. She opened her mouth and slid half of the finger sandwich in. Oh Christ. How could he be expected to stay composed when she did things like that?

Cool it, Carter.

"Mmm, so good," she said and slipped the last bite in. Just like that, his mind returned to sex.

What the hell was wrong with him? He was a lawyer for God's sake. Composed. Careful. Logical.

So why the hell was he still thinking about the two of them naked when he knew getting involved with a girl like her was all wrong? Perhaps it was because he was high up in the mountains and not getting enough oxygen to fuel his brain. Yeah, that had to be the logical conclusion.

But then she dropped her napkin and bent over to get it, and therein laid the true reason why he couldn't think rationally. She was hot.

Looking for a distraction, he asked, "Why do you have so much food? Were you expecting company?"

She frowned. "It was for the shelter. I spent days

preparing it." She shrugged easily, like she was brushing it off. "If we don't get out soon, I'll just freeze what we can't eat and start again. I like to bring fresh food." Smile restored, she looked at him. "I guess it's a good thing you took the wrong road. Now I have someone to share this with."

Did she always see the bright in everything? Honest to God, a sweet thing like her was probably a regular on Santa's nice list.

"But I'm not staying."

"Yeah, you said that already," she responded, like she didn't quite believe him.

He looked around the small cabin with the big window overlooking the snow peaked mountains. "So do you live here?" he asked.

"No, this cabin belongs to Stone Cliff Resort, and they're letting me use it to for a few months while I write my thesis. My family lives in town, and I'll be joining them for the holidays."

"Your thesis is on wolf behavior?" he asked, interested to know more about her.

She nodded. "Yeah, pack animals fascinate me, but I'm mostly interested in the lone wolf."

At the mention of the lone wolf, he looked out her window and thought he saw a flash of blue. But then he shook his head. That white wolf with the strange blue eyes had to be long gone by now, and he believed in logic, not legends. Besides, if what she said was true, and the wolf would give him what he needed, he'd damn well be on a plane home right now. Because what he really *needed* was to be in his apartment, alone, away from the holidays and what they made him remember...*feel*.

"What is it about the lone wolf that interests you?" he asked.

She took a drink of her milk and wiped her mouth. "I

study how those pushed from the pack, or those who remove themselves for their own reasons, try to start their own family or work their way into an already established one." She played with a crumb on her plate, then looked back at him, a real sincerity in her eyes when she added, "It's not natural for any animal to be alone. Some think they don't need anyone, but I can tell you they really are miserable deep down."

"I don't know if I believe that." Hell, he'd removed himself emotionally from all those around him, and he was doing just fine. "I'm sure there are exceptions to the rule."

She blinked up at him. "You think?"

"Sure." He gave an easy roll of his shoulders. "I like being alone."

Her brows arched. "Yeah? So you live alone?"

"Yeah, in a high-rise in the city."

"And you like that?"

He nodded. "Which is why I want to get home." Feeling oddly uncomfortable as she studied him with those big brown eyes—in much the same manner as Mayor Walker stared at him—he grabbed his glass and drained the last of his milk.

"Hmm."

"What?" he asked.

"Nothing." She reached for the carton of milk. "Here, have some more." She poured then looked past his shoulders through the glass window. "It's getting dark."

"I should probably get going before it gets too late." He pushed away from the table and she jumped up.

"Hang on." She darted to the back porch area and came back with a man's coat, a hat, and a pair of boots. "You can't get back into your wet coat and shoes."

"Thanks." He walked to the door and shrugged into the heavy brown coat and boots. Another perfect fit. "I'll send these back after I get home." He took another look around at her cozy cottage and gave her dogs a quick pat on the head when they came rushing over like they were expecting him to take them for a walk. Their tails thumped against the cupboards excitedly. "Listen, thanks for everything." When a log on the fire splintered and another Christmas tune came on the radio, he turned and reached for the door.

As soon as his hand curled around the knob, Josie asked, "What are you doing?"

He spun back to face her. "Going to my car."

"Didn't you want me to drive you?" She grabbed her coat off the back of the sofa and pulled it on.

"I figured I could walk."

"What's with you, City?" Why would you do that when I have a perfectly good truck sitting outside?"

"I'm not about to ask you—"

"I know you're far away from home, so I'll cut you some slack, but just remember, around these parts, we all help each other. All you have to do is ask." She pulled on her boots and pushed past him. He tightened his scarf against the blowing wind and raced after her.

He climbed into the truck, and when she sat there staring at the dashboard, her lips twisted into a frown, he asked, "What?"

"It doesn't look like you're going anywhere."

He leaned into her and looked at the dashboard. "What are you talking about?"

She tried to turn the key over, but nothing happened. "The truck won't start."

"What the hell?"

She nodded like everything made sense. "The wolf," she said matter-of-factly. "It's keeping you here."

"I don't believe in your legend, Josie. It's probably dead because it's freezing out and you didn't plug in your block heater." He looked out at the driving snow. "Besides, it's still light enough for me to walk." Barely, but if he hurried...

"Okay, suit yourself," she said. Was she always so easygoing, taking everything in stride? "Be careful out there." She jumped from the truck, and he plugged in her block heater as she turned back toward her cottage.

"Thanks again," he yelled over the wind, and she gave him a little wave. He pulled his hat down lower over his eyes and was about to turn into the breeze when he saw Josie dart around the side of the cabin, a huge gust practically lifting her off the ground.

Where the hell was she going?

He looked at the road, then back to her cottage. He waited a moment. She didn't reappear. Dammit. He drove his hands into his pockets and followed her tracks. He caught site of her near a woodpile, half covered by a tarp. He watched her struggle with a few heavy logs, slipping a little on the ice and getting a face full of snow. If he stopped to help her, he'd never make it to the road before dark.

Nice guys finish last, Carter.

She loaded more wood into her arms, until she couldn't even see over the pile. Mumbling curses under his breath, he trudged toward her.

"Here, let me help." He grabbed the top logs from her. She blinked those beautiful brown eyes at him and it felt like a fist to the gut. How could anyone be so sweet and innocent, wholesome, and sexy at the same time? She wet her mouth, licking snow from her lips, and all he could think about was leaning forward for a little taste. But the last thing he should be doing is getting wrapped up in a girl who just might want more from a guy who didn't do emotions. He was on the fast track to making partner at his firm, and she was a complication he didn't need in his life.

"You shouldn't be trying to carry so much." He tore off one glove and brushed the snow from her cheeks. "Where I come from, we call this the lazy man's load."

Breathing hard, she followed him inside with the two logs he'd left in her arms. "I didn't want to have to make too many trips. It's cold out." She dropped the wood into the box and brushed the dirt from her small hands.

Carter put his logs on top of hers, but the box was far from being full. "Do you need much more?"

She frowned and put her hands on her hips. "I need to fill it if I want to keep the fire going until morning."

"Fine, let's hurry, though."

"That's what I was trying to do."

They went back outside, and after a few more trips, they finally had the box full. He helped her with the tarp, then he glanced at the sky, which was now black. Shit. He looked at her and caught her grinning.

"What?"

"Do you believe me now?" she asked.

"If you're taking about the legend, and the wolf keeping me here, then no. This is just an unfortunate set of coincidences."

"Hmmm."

"What?"

"I didn't take you for the type of guy who believed in coincidences."

13

As the morning sun climbed the mountains, Josie tiptoed around the living room, trying not to wake Carter as he slept quietly on the sofa. With his blankets half off, she caught a glimpse of his bare chest and navy blue boxers. She gifted herself with a longer look, taking in his strong profile, long hard body, and the hand he had on Bear's head, like he'd fallen asleep petting him. For a guy who didn't like dogs, he sure seemed to have bonded with hers. He might be a badass lawyer by trade, but underneath his wool coat and hard exterior, there was a softer side to him, one he went to great lengths to hide.

She looked at her big Christmas tree. Last night, she'd left the lights on, but sometime after she'd gone to bed, he must have pulled the plug. She plugged it back in then padded to her room. She rooted around inside the closet and grabbed a fresh pair of jeans and a T-shirt, thankful that Jack kept a spare set of clothes at the cottage for when they went snow-mobile riding. Walking quietly back to the main room, she placed them on the table bedside Carter. When her coffee maker beeped, she darted to her kitchen and took two cups from the cupboard, leaving one on the counter for her sleeping lone wolf. After doctoring hers, she pulled on her vest and hat and called for her dogs.

They slipped out the back porch, and as Sasha and Bear took off to play in the snow, she lowered herself into her Adirondack chair and sipped coffee as the sun climbed higher in the sky. She lifted her chin, letting the long rays warm her face.

"Hey," a sexy voice said from the doorway.

She turned to see Carter standing there, raking his fingers through his mussed hair. A burst of heat moved through her as she looked at him, reminding her she hadn't had a boyfriend since her first year of college. Carter was right. She did spend too much time alone in the woods, and honestly, she really missed being with someone. She'd been studying hard for the last four years, but the truth was, it had been a long time since a man interested her—especially like this one did.

She let her eyes trail the length of him. Dressed in the clothes she'd laid out for him, he looked warm, relaxed, sexy, and it was pretty much all she could do to keep herself from running for the mistletoe. There was no denying that Carter Reed was drop dead gorgeous, and she wouldn't mind getting to know him better—even though he seemed hell bent on getting out of town.

"I see you found Jack's clothes," she said, her breath turning to fog in the cold morning. "I knew they'd fit perfectly."

"Yeah, thanks." He drove his hands in his pockets. "Ah, speaking of Jack, is he going to show up here and kick my ass?"

"Why would he do that?"

"You, me, alone in the cabin. I mean if you were my girl—"

She burst out laughing. "Jack is the oldest of my three brothers, and I'm a big girl, City. Who I have for a sleepover is my business, and my family respects that."

"So you don't have a boyfriend?"

"No, I don't."

"And sleepovers? Do you have a lot of them?"

"That is *my* business." She bent forward, grabbed a fist full of snow and tossed it at him. "Now grab a coffee and come on out. You're making me miss the best part of the day."

He disappeared inside for a moment, then came back with Jack's coat and hat on and a steaming cup of java.

Looking sleepy, he sank into the seat beside her and scrubbed his chin. "Why are you up so early?"

She nodded toward the mountain and he followed her gaze. "I bet you don't get this view from your high-rise." She exhaled a happy sigh and wondered how anyone could live in the city. When she was away at college those last four years, all she wanted to do was get back to her beloved mountains. "Gorgeous, isn't it?"

He was quiet for a long time, then he said, "Yeah..."

When she heard something in his voice, something wistful and longing, she angled her head to see him and realized he was looking at her. Her heart gave a little start when their eyes met. Carter cleared his throat and quickly shifted his focus, taking a big drink of his coffee.

"The road's clear. Looks like you're free to go," she said, but since the wolf had stranded him here she had a feeling he wouldn't be leaving until after the holidays.

"Really? When did that happen?"

"My dad and Jack did it last night. They called earlier to let me know. You must have been pretty tired. The ringer didn't even wake you."

"Must be all this fresh mountain air."

"Oh," she added, "and they towed your car back to the

rental place. Dad has your bags."

He gave her a puzzled look. "All this happened and it's only what..." He paused and looked at his watch. "Five in the morning."

She laughed. "That's that way it works in small towns. We ask for help. We get help."

"I guess I should get going then," he said, but he continued to sit there, watching her dogs play in the distance. She looked him over and noticed that his shoulders didn't seem quite as tense as yesterday. She liked this relaxed Carter. Liked him very much.

"What's your hurry?"

"Tomorrow is Christmas Eve," he said.

She nodded, thinking how she and her brothers all gathered at her folks' place on the twenty-fourth for food, music, and laughter. "Right, and your family is probably having a big gathering and are anxious to have you home."

"I don't have a family," he said quickly, too quickly. Then, as if he'd said too much, he began backtracking. "I mean. I had a lot of families over the years..." He stopped and took another drink of coffee.

"Come on." Josie set her coffee down and jumped up.

"Where?" he asked.

Carter followed her as she rounded the corner of the cottage. "For a ride." She stepped under the awning and pulled the cover off the snowmobile.

His mouth dropped open. "You mean to tell me this was here all along? I could have used it to get to my car."

"Oh," she answered. "I never thought, and of course, you didn't ask."

"How could I ask if I didn't know?"

She nodded. "True."

He stepped closer, his body crowding hers. "Maybe it's not the wolf keeping me here, after all. Maybe there really wasn't a log obstructing the road, and you didn't plug your block heater in on purpose."

She laughed and poked him in the chest. "And here you thought *I* was the one who should be worried about *you*."

His hand closed over hers, big, warm, and strong. "So you admit you *are* holding me hostage, Josie?" His voice deepened. Josie swallowed as the air around them charged, became sexual.

"I not admitting to anything," she said, sounding completely breathless as his big hand swallowed hers whole.

He dipped his head. "I'm a lawyer. I have ways of making you talk."

"I don't know, City. I can be pretty tight-lipped when I want to be."

"Tight-lipped is my specialty."

"Maybe, but I bet you've never come across someone as stubborn as me before."

His blue eyes darkened. "You could be right."

"I'm like Fort Knox."

"I like a challenge."

She swallowed against the dryness in her throat as their teasing banter turned sexual. She suspected Carter rarely showed this playful, flirty side of himself, and she had to admit she liked it. She liked it a lot.

"Do you now?" she asked.

"Yeah, because I'd really like to get to the bottom of why you're holding me hostage." He leaned closer, and his warm breath washed over her face. "What do you want from me, Josie?"

With his mouth only inches from hers, she was sure he was going to kiss her, and dammit, she really wanted him to, but her dog came running up to them, breaking the moment.

Carter stiffened and stepped back, and as she thought about how close he'd come to kissing her, it raised one very important question. What *did* she want from him? She'd already decided she'd like to get to know him better, but did better mean intimate? Yeah, she was pretty sure it did.

They both stood there for a second, and when Bear nudged her, nipping at the bottom of her pant legs like he always did when he wanted to play, she said, "We'll have to save the interrogation for later." He continued to stand there, poker straight, staring at her. She started the snowmobile and pulled her gloves from her pockets. "Get on."

He looked a bit hesitant. "You sure you know how to drive this thing?"

"Are you telling me you've never been on a snowmobile before?" He nodded. "Don't worry, City. Tight-lipped is your specialty." She revved the engine. "This is mine."

Still looking a bit unsure, he hopped on behind her and slid his hands around her waist, linking them together over her stomach. A warm shiver moved through her, and it became abundantly clear how aware they were of each other and how nice it was to be held by him.

She took off toward the woods surrounding the cottage, the freshly fallen snow clinging to the branches and glistening in the sunlight. Her dogs followed, barking and darting in and out of the trees. She went a little faster, and his hands tightened on her stomach. She climbed higher up the mountain and stopped when she came to a flat area. Tapping his hand, she gestured with her head and they both looked at the gorgeous view below. Then she pointed to the lone set of wolf tracks.

"Do you think that's your wolf?" she asked loudly over the roar of the engine.

He squeezed her waist. "I don't have a wolf."

Laughing, she headed back down the hill and drove to the cottage. She pulled under the awning, powered down the machine, and turned to him. "Fun, huh?"

"Yeah," he said, grinning like a kid on Christmas morning. "Except you drive like a maniac."

"I have three older brothers, remember. I had to keep up. You can take it for a run tomorrow if you like."

"I won't be here tomorrow."

"Oh right."

"Why do you say that like you don't believe me?"

"I believe you." At least she believed that he believed it.

He climbed off and she followed him inside the cottage. He pulled his hat off and stood there like he didn't know what to do next. Her heart pinched, because as he glanced around her decorated cottage, there was something very sweet about him, something very vulnerable.

Gathering herself, she said, "I'll drive you to get your bags and drop you off at the airport. But first, we need to eat breakfast."

"Do you think your truck will work?"

"I guess we'll find out." She flicked on the radio to fill the cottage with Christmas music.

A pained expression came over his face. "Do you have to listen to Christmas music twenty-four-seven?"

"You don't like Christmas music?"

"Something like that."

"You really are Scrooge, aren't you? You don't like dogs, you don't music, you don't like lights."

"I never said anything about lights."

"You didn't have to. I left the tree plugged in last night because I thought you might enjoy it, but this morning, the lights were off."

"Maybe I couldn't sleep because they were too bright."

"So you're telling me you do like lights."

"Well, no."

She laughed and pointed to the bathroom. "Go get a shower while I whip us up something to eat."

He shot a glance toward the front door and froze when he looked through the windowpane.

"What?" she asked.

"I thought..." He let his words fall off. "Nothing. I probably should just get going."

She pointed to his hair. "With that hat head? I don't know, City. They might not let you on the plane looking like that."

"Oh, you're one to talk," he shot back, his hand going to her messy locks. "Have you ever even heard of a comb?"

He raked his fingers through her short hair, and she sucked in a breath, the heat from touch traveling all the way to her toes, stopping at a few erogenous zones along the way.

He pulled his hand back like it had been burned. "Oh... I...sorry."

Her heart thudded a little faster. "You don't have to be sorry. If you want to touch my hair, you can touch my hair." She looked at him and wondered if there were any other places he'd like to touch, because yeah, she could think of a few. It had been a long time since she'd been with somebody, and while she wasn't the kind of girl to jump into bed with a random man, her heart told her Carter was anything but. There was something very special about him, something very good in his heart.

He peeled off his coat and jerked his thumb toward the shower. "I...ah...I should probably grab that shower."

"Don't use all the hot water."

"I'll probably just use cold," he mumbled under his breath as he turned and walked away, his tight ass dragging her focus. Her thoughts shifted direction as she continued to stare, and she couldn't help but think it had been a long time since she'd asked Santa for something special under her tree. Since she was pretty sure Carter was going to be around for the holidays, she couldn't think of anyone else she'd rather unwrap.

14

Carter sat beside Josie in her truck, happy that the engine had turned over, and listened to her sing off-key to a Christmas song. Even though he hated the song, he couldn't help but grin, especially when she messed up the words and kept right along. He'd never quite met anyone like her. Easy-going, easy to be with, always taking everything in stride. Basically, she was the opposite of him in almost every way. They clearly weren't compatible, which made him wonder why he'd felt a spark of jealousy when he thought Jack was her boyfriend.

"What?" she asked, a wide smile on her face.

"You sing as well as you drive."

"Hey." She wacked him and punched up the volume, just to annoy him, he was sure. "If you think you can do better, let me hear it."

"Don't think so."

"Then zip it." She ran her finger across her lips, lips that kept drawing his attention, even though it wasn't in his best interests. He shifted, his jeans suddenly feeling a little too tight in the crotch area.

As they approached town, he grabbed his phone and called up the flights. "Looks like I can get out of here mid-afternoon."

"Do you want me to drop you off now?" she asked, and again, he couldn't help but think how she was placating him, because he got the feeling she didn't believe he'd be going anywhere anytime soon.

He glanced in the back seat at all the food she had for the shelter. It was a lot to carry, and she was such a little girl. With a few hours to spare, he supposed he had time to help. After all, she'd come to his rescue and had given him a place to stay.

"I can give you a hand with this first," he said.

"Sounds good."

Her head bobbed to the beat, and before he realized what he was doing, he was tapping his fingers on the dashboard. Shit. He pulled his hand back but caught the smirk on Josie's face.

She parked along the street. Carter climbed out and noticed the pet store and all the puppies in the window. He could only imagine how many little kids would be asking for one of those purebreds for Christmas, and how many would be left disappointed.

He walked around back of the SUV to meet Josie. "Grab those two containers," she said as she shuffled the boxes around. Just then, her phone pinged. She pulled it from her back pocket and grinned. "Dad's on his way. He's going to dress as Santa and meet with the kids. Hang on, I'll ask him to bring your luggage."

She punched the message, then stuffed the phone into her pocket as he gathered up the plastic containers full of turkey.

"Do you do this every year?" he asked.

"Sure do. My dad's the mayor, and he likes to take care of those in his town. My brothers and I all help out the best we can. They leave the cooking to me." She laughed and grabbed a container full of stuffing and a bag of rolls. "Because no one wants a charcoal turkey that looks like a sacrificial offering on their dinner plate." Carter stood on the curb as she trudged down the long driveway toward the back entrance of the church. When she realized he wasn't following, she glanced over her shoulder. "Aren't you coming?"

"Your father is the mayor?"

"Yeah, I thought you knew that."

"How would I know that? You didn't tell me."

"You didn't ask."

"Why would I ask?"

She shrugged and shifted the bag of rolls in her arms. "Beats me."

He nodded toward the old, rundown church. "You said we were going to a shelter, but this is the church my client bought, isn't it? The one the town uses as a food bank?"

"Yeah, shelter, food bank. Same thing. Now come on, we have some hungry people to feed."

Shit.

He'd never personally visited the property, and even though the church was the last place he wanted to be, he followed along. She used her shoulder to push open the heavy back door, and a burst of heat washed over them as they stepped inside. Laugher could be heard as kids played and ran around the big open room while their parents stood in line to get them food.

"Hey Josie," a pretty, middle-age woman wearing a hair net called out.

Josie placed her food on the counter and dropped a kiss on the woman's cheek. "Mom, this is Carter. He's staying with me for a few days. Carter this is Mary, my mom."

Josie took the containers from him, and he held his hand out to her mother, but she shooed it away and wrapped him in a hug. "Carter, it's nice to meet you. Josie told her father you'd be staying awhile when she called him last night about the road."

He shifted, feeling a little uncomfortable. "Nice to meet you," he said. "And I only stayed the one night. She was kind enough to take me in and offer her sofa." In fact, it was also kind of her father and brother to tow his car to the rental place as well. He couldn't image why they'd do that, for him of all people. "I'm heading to the airport in a few minutes."

"Well, before you go, would you two mind setting up the Santa chair? It's in the back room and your father is on his way." She smiled at all the children playing, a warm motherly look that had Carter's heart pinching. She clasped her hands together. "Look at them all. They're so excited to see Santa."

"Let us grab the rest of the food," Josie said. "Then we'll get the chair."

They made a few more trips to the truck, then headed to the back storage room. When he saw the plush Santa Chair, Carter scrubbed his face and asked, "Are you sure this is a good idea?"

She crinkled her nose. "Bringing the chair out?"

"No, I mean, all those kids asking Santa for a gift. I mean...they don't have..."

She blinked up at him, the warmth in her eyes doing the strangest things to him. "What they have is belief, Carter," she said, and he realized she'd used his real name for the first time.

"Isn't your dad kind of setting them up for disappointment?"

She went quiet for a moment, her glance moving over his face, those big eyes of hers assessing him in a way that made him feel...made him remember that he wasn't worthy of anyone's love.

"Is that how you see it?" she asked.

"It's not how I see it, Josie. It's how it is."

A sadness backlit her eyes as she touched his cheek. In the softest voice, she whispered, "I'm sorry."

His throat tightened and she stepped back. "Hey, I'm fine. I was just thinking—"

"About the kids. I know. You're a good guy, Carter."

Good guy? Hardly.

These folks were all going to be left in the cold because of him. "Don't be so sure about that," he mumbled and grabbed the chair. "I got this."

"Are you sure? It's heavy."

He carried it into the main room, and the kids starting clapping and jumping up and down when they saw it.

"Santa's coming! Santa's coming!" They all shouted in unison. "I'm going to ask for a puppy," one of the little boys said. "I want a dolly," a girl shouted.

He looked at his watch as Mary came up to them. "I have one more thing to ask before you head out. Would you mind running to Johnson's convenience to grab a few more boxes of candy canes? I think we're going to need them."

Carter looked at his watch. "Okay," he said. "I still have time."

They stepped outside and when they reached the sidewalk, Josie slipped on a patch of ice. "Whoa!" she yelled.

Carter put his arm around her and held her to him. "You okay?" he asked.

"My hero," she said, blinking up at him.

"I'm nobody's hero."

Instead of answering, she snuggled in tighter and stayed in his arms as they walked down the sidewalk. He slowed in front of the pet store and looked at the cute pup clawing at the window.

"I think he likes you," Josie said. Then she nudged him. "Too bad you don't like dogs."

They reached the convenience store, and the bell overhead jingled when he pulled the door open. The girl working the cash register smiled at them, and an elderly gentleman behind the pharmacy counter lit up when he saw Josie.

"Josie," he said. "I heard you had trouble on your road last night."

"Yeah, but dad and Jack fixed it." She pointed to Carter, then grabbed a couple boxes of candy canes from the shelf. "This is Carter. He's staying with me for a few days."

"Actually, I'm headed to the airport in a few minutes," Carter corrected. Josie smiled at him and handed him the boxes. She grabbed a few more and started humming to the Christmas music playing from an overhead speaker.

Mr. Johnson frowned. "I guess you haven't heard."

"Heard what?" Carter asked.

"The airport is covered in fog. Nothing coming. Nothing going. I think you might be stuck here a little longer." He placed his hands on the counter and gruffed. "They built that damn airport in a fishbowl. No wonder the place is always getting fogged in."

A strange, uneasy feeling moved into Carter's stomach. Okay, this was getting weird.

"Thanks for the update," Josie said. "You tell Elaine we said hello, and Merry Christmas to you all."

Carter followed her to the front. "He's kidding, right?"

"Why would he kid about that?"

"Josie, this is strange."

She stopped and turned to him. "When are you going to start believing me?"

He looked out the window and saw a flash of blue. "It's a little far-fetched."

"Not so far," she said and dropped the boxes on the counter. "You might as well start accepting that you're going to be spending Chrisms with me."

"No, I'm not," he said a little too harshly. Christ, she was too temping, too sweet, and he needed to be away from her sooner rather than later. Otherwise, he was pretty sure he was going to kiss the hell out of her. And he wasn't so sure he could stop there. "I'm going home. One way or another, I'm going home."

She turned to him, a hurt look on her face. "Is being here with me so bad, Carter?"

Feeling like a world-class prick as she turned those dark eyes on him, he said, "No. I didn't mean that. I just...I have to get home."

"Why?"

"Because I do."

"That hardly seems like a good enough reason." She pulled her wallet from her purse. "You said no one was waiting for you, so what's the rush?"

The cashier rang them in and put the candy into bags as Carter pulled out his phone and checked his flight. Sure enough, everything was delayed due to fog.

"I'll check into Stone Cliff. I'm not going to put you out any more than I have."

"Okay, suit yourself, but I don't think you'll be able to get a room."

"Why not?"

She shrugged easily. "They go to minimum staff this time of year, and if you're not booked already, you likely won't get booked."

He called up the website and phoned registration. After a quick chat with the receptionist, he hung up. "Shit."

She puckered her lips. Christ, he really wished she wouldn't do that. "No rooms?"

"No."

"So you have two choices. Stay with me, or sleep on an airport bench until the flights start again. I'm guessing, since you hate the idea of staying with me, that you'll—"

"I never said that. I just…never mind."

"Okay."

He followed her outside, and she swung the bags as she continued to hum. They walked past the pet store, and as they approached the church, and saw the front doors wide open, she headed toward them.

"Dad must be here," she said excitedly. "Come on, we'll get your bags." She rushed up the steps and he kept pace behind her. When they reached the top landing, she stopped abruptly and he crashed into her.

"What?" He put his mouth close to her ear and was sure a shiver moved through her. Yeah, whatever this thing was between them, she felt it every bit as much as he did. But dammit, he was not going to act on it. Now way. No how.

"My brother," she said pointing.

Carter glanced up and spotted a guy and girl kissing in the doorway. Josie sagged against him. "That's Katee Fraser. She's been after Jack for a long time."

"Looks like she's finally caught him," he whispered.

She gave a happy sigh. "Christmas really is magical."

"Maybe," he said, taking note of the mistletoe. *Or maybe not.*

As soon as they stopped kissing, Josie ran toward them, Carter following her. "Hey big bro," she said, grinning. "You got something to say?"

He pointed upward. "Yeah, your turn."

Josie's eyes lit when she spotted the mistletoe over the door. "Oh!"

Dressed as Santa's helper, Katee took off to help the mayor, and eyes that mirrored Josie's met Carter's. Jack grinned and folded his arms. "What are you waiting for, little sis? Time to kiss your boyfriend."

"Wait, we're not..." Carter stepped back. "She's not..."

"She's not what?" Jack asked, his grin widening. "Good enough for a city boy like you?"

Christ, was this whole town conspiring against him? "No, that's not what I meant." He looked at Josie. Sweet Josie, who he wanted to kiss in the worst way. But it was a bad idea. She was a nice girl who made him want to ask for things he knew better than to ask for.

Josie went up onto her toes. "He's not going to leave us alone until you kiss me. So let's just get this over with."

Carter pulled her to him. "Fine," he said, and pressed his mouth to hers for a quick, hurried kiss, knowing anything else would be too tempting, too dangerous. But the second he felt her soft lips on his, felt the way her body warmed in his arms, he forgot why getting close was a bad idea. She put her arms around his shoulders and held tight, and as her body fit against his, molding like a well-worn glove, he deepened the kiss, wanting, no *needing*, more. Her lips parted, and despite their audience of one, he slipped his tongue inside. *Oh God*. She was so sweet, so warm and welcoming, he almost forgot they were standing in a church, in a town he was desperate to escape.

Jack cleared his throat and Carter broke the kiss. With his arms still around Josie, he stood there staring at here, taking note of the desire reflecting in her eyes. Oh, Jesus, she wanted this, too. No way could he crash on her sofa knowing she was only a few feet away and wanted this as much as he did.

Walk away, Carter. Just walk away.

"Josie," he whispered.

"Yeah," she said, sounding breathless.

Go to the airport, Carter.

Even though it went against his own best interests, he said, "About your sofa...if the offer is still open..."

Shit.

"It is," she said quickly.

As Carter looked at sweet and sexy Josie, taking in the warm flush on her cheeks, he knew spending the holidays with a nice girl like her was a bad idea—a really fucking bad idea—which made him wonder what is was about her—this town—that had him acting so out of character.

15

Josie could feel Carter's eyes on her as she drove them back to her cottage. The glances he kept aiming her way had her temperature jumping a few degrees, despite the cold mountain air. Honest to God, the intense look on his face made her feel all jittery inside, all hyped up.

Fully aware of the increased sexual tension between them since the kiss, she wet her bottom lip, still tasting him on her mouth. There was no denying that the second her lips had touched his, it had done something to him—to her. He'd dropped his guard when he pulled her to him, and she caught the deeper emotion in his eyes as their tongues tangled. Truthfully, she didn't know him very well, but she was certain of two things—he wanted her every bit as much as she wanted him, but there was something holding him back. Perhaps that something had everything to do with his white wolf, and why it was keeping him here with her.

She pulled into her driveway and slammed the truck into Park. "I have to take the dogs out for a walk," she said, trying for casual even though her blood was pounding hard through her body. "Then I'll make us something to eat."

"I'll help."

He walked to the house with her and stayed so close she could smell her soap on his skin. She unlocked her door and he reached around her to open it. His body pressed against hers, and she drew a breath to center herself. The dogs barked and took off around the back of the house. Josie turned to follow and didn't miss the hunger in Carter's eyes as he looked at her. Her hands brushed his as she walked alongside him. When they reached the backyard, Josie made a snowball and threw it. Bear chased after it, catching it in his mouth.

"Hey Sasha," Carter called out. Sasha turned his way and he tossed a snowball. She barked and ran after it, and the smile on Carter's face just about melted Josie's heart.

"What?" he asked, when he caught her looking at him.

"I think you like my dogs," she teased.

He leaned into her, his breath warm on her face. "Then you would be wrong."

"Really?"

"Yeah, really," he said.

"I think you're lying, and you know what we do to liars around these parts?" she asked.

"What?"

She cupped a fistful of snow and tossed it at him, catching him right between the eyes.

He sputtered and wiped his face on his sleeve. When he looked back at her, there was a teasing gleam in his eyes. "Oh, it's on now," he said and ran after her.

Josie squealed and took off but didn't get very far before Carter scooped her up and spun her around. A second later, they were both flat out on the ground, Carter's body pressing hers into the wet snow.

He grabbed her arms and pinned them above her head.

Heat moved into his eyes as he gazed at her mouth. She swiped her tongue over her bottom lip, waiting for him to kiss her again—needing him to kiss her again. His Adam's apple bobbed as he swallowed, and a tortured, almost conflicted look crossed his handsome face.

She waited a moment longer. The kisses didn't come. "Carter?"

"Yeah?"

"Is there something you want?" He didn't answer. Instead he looked at her with those haunted eyes of his. "Because, you know, if you want something, all you have to do is ask," she said.

They exchanged a long, heated look and he shifted on top of her. His erection pressed into her leg, and she moved beneath him, her body growing hot despite the wet snow seeping soaking clothes. A cool breeze whipped over them, and a tremor raced through her. But it had had more to do with Carter's hard body than the arctic wind.

Her dogs barked in the near distance, breaking the moment, and Carter's body stiffened. "We...ah...we should probably get inside," he said, his voice deeper than it was seconds ago.

"Sure," she said.

With his guard back in place, he climbed off her and grabbed her hand to pull her up. Her body collided with his, and she heard a groan catch in his throat.

"Everything okay?" she asked, knowing full well this thing between them, this pull, was getting harder and harder to ignore, and while she was ready to act on it, there was something holding Carter back.

"Yeah."

She whistled for her dogs and they came running toward her. Entering through the porch, she shrugged out of her coat and left it on the floor as her dogs sauntered to their beds near the fire.

She touched her damp pant legs. "I should probably get out of these wet clothes."

"Yeah, me too." He jerked his thumb toward the door. "I'll grab my bags from the truck."

Carter left through the porch door, and Josie darted to her room to get changed. Her body was still on hyper drive—so darn needy for Carter's touch, his mouth—but she suspected if she wanted him in her bed, she'd have to make the first move. She had no idea what tomorrow held for them, and while she wasn't a girl who took sex lightly, tonight she knew what she wanted and feared she'd regret letting him walk out of her life without doing something about it.

Deciding to go for it, she pulled on a short nightgown, one that barely covered her backside, and grabbed her prettiest Christmas panties from her dresser.

She heard Carter rustling around in the other room and opened her bedroom door to find him pulling on his dry clothes. The second she looked at him, her body began burning up and she knew she was making the right decision. She hadn't known him for long, but being with him felt right —in her head and in her heart. Only question was, how could she go about getting him to drop his guard with her and let him know it was okay to ask for what he wanted?

She thought about that for a moment then walked past him to the woodstove. "So, about this interrogation," she began as she bent forward to toss another log into the hearth, fully aware that she was giving him an up close and personal view of candy canes on her lacy panties.

"What...uh...what about it?" he asked.

She wiggled slightly and grabbed the poker to stoke the fire. "Did you still want to get to the *bottom* of matters?"

He cursed under his breath. "What are you doing, Josie?"

Josie stood and turned to him. "I thought we might continue where we left off this afternoon. You did tell me tight-lipped was your specialty and that you liked a challenge. I'm simply interested in your techniques, you know, in all the ways you can make me talk."

Or moan.

His nostrils flared and the muscles along his jaw rippled as he clenched down. She closed the short distance between them and touched his face, running her hands over his sexy stubble. A strange stillness settled over him when she pressed her body against his.

"Jesus Christ, Josie," he said, his voice so strained it was difficult to understand him.

"What is it, Carter? Is there something you want?"

He gripped her hair and pushed it from her face, a low sound in his throat as he pressed his forehead to hers. "I...I..."

"If there is something you want, all you have to do is ask," she whispered.

"Josie..." he growled, a note of desperation in that one word as his hands fisted her hair.

Even though he couldn't seem to say the words, she could read the want in his eyes, feel it in his body. Deciding that was good enough for now, she stepped back, gripped the hem of her nightshirt, and peeled it over her head. He swept his gaze down the length of her and groaned low in his throat.

"Oh, fuck." As something inside him seemed to give, he wrapped his hand around her head to drag her mouth to his, and her body trembled almost controllably. "Just once, Josie. Just tonight. That's all I can do."

"Just once," she murmured, her brain barely registering his words as his hands left her face to slide down toward her waist. He gripped her hips and pulled her against him until her small breasts were crushed against the soft fabric of his dress shirt. Desire twisted inside her.

"You are so gorgeous," he said, his mouth leaving hers to go to the soft hollow of her throat. He flicked his tongue out and traced the long length of her neck, the soft blade teasing the sensitive spot that always made her quiver.

She raked her fingers through his hair as he pressed his nose to her skin. He drew a sharp breath. "And you smell so fucking good," he murmured. He sank to his knees, and a barrage of sensations rocketed through her when his mouth found her nipple.

"Oh, yes," she murmured and arched into him. He licked lightly and splayed his big hands over the small of her back, the warmth of his skin burning through her body. His mouth went lower, and he licked her sex through her candy cane panties.

"Sweet as candy," he murmured. "But they're in the way of what I really want to taste."

She rocked against his mouth and he gripped the lace and lowered it to her ankles. She lifted her feet for him, and he tossed the scrap of material away. Behind them, Bear flipped onto his back and let loose a loud yawn. Carter froze and looked up at her, and for a minute, she thought he was going to retreat.

"Bedroom," he said.

She nodded and he climbed to his feet. She was about to grab his hand and take him to her room, but he scooped her up, used his foot to push her bedroom door open, and dropped her onto the bed.

"Oh," she said as he stood there staring at her, looking so hot and sexy she began tingling from head to toe.

His hands went to his buttons, and she was sure his fingers were shaking as he pulled them open. He shrugged out of the shirt, and she couldn't seem to take her eyes off his body. Lean. Hard. Cut.

Mine for the night.

"Everything okay?" he asked, his hands going to his belt.

Her gaze shifted back to his face and she tried not to sound as breathless as she felt when she said, "Everything is better than okay."

He grinned. "So you like what you see?"

She crooked her finger. "Actually, I see better with my hands."

"All righty then," he murmured, and he made quick work of his pants. "Maybe I was wrong about you all along. Maybe you're not on Santa's nice list."

"Oh, I am. Come here and I'll show you how nice I can be."

Carter slid over her, his weight pushing her into the mattress as he settled his hard body on top of hers. She put her arms around him and feathered her fingers over his muscles as his mouth found hers. A moan caught in her throat as they traded soft kisses, his hands gripping fistfuls of her hair. Her body warmed against his, and her toes curled as his erection pressed into her leg.

His mouth left hers and slid over her throat until he reached her breasts. His lips closed around one hard nipple. She arched into him and ran her hands through his hair. He shifted to his side and caressed her skin, soft, barely touching, as he gently introduced himself to her body. His knuckle nudged her clit as his hand went to her thighs to widen them. He slipped a hand between her knees and pushed them open. She swallowed as he stroked her inner thighs, his fingers leisurely climbing higher and higher. His movements were slow, deliberate, the most intimate thing she'd ever experienced. He drew her nipple deeper into her mouth, and pleasure rippled through her as his fingers found her clit. He brushed so lightly, so delicately. Her hips came off the bed, seeking more.

"Oh, God," she cried out and grabbed his shoulders, loving the way his muscles rippled beneath her hands. His mouth left her breasts and he slid downward, positioning himself between her legs. He lifted his chin to meet her eyes, and she caught the intense look on his face as he widened her thighs even more. The heat in his eyes licked over her body in ways that made her aware of how much he wanted her—how much she wanted him. She knew this was all happening fast for her, but the truth was, this was Carter. Deep down, she knew he was a good guy, and she'd never needed to be touched by anyone quite like the way she needed to be touched by him.

He lowered his head, and her breath grew shallow at that first sweet touch of his tongue. The heat from his mouth boiled her blood as the wet tip skated across the seam of her lips. He trailed his tongue all the way from the bottom to the top, then widened her with the soft blade. Sparks shot through her body at the sweet invasion.

She drew a shaky breath and gripped his shoulder. "Carter," she murmured, her nails digging into his skin.

He licked slowly, softly, and wanting, no *needing* more, she lifted her hips to hurry him along. But he pressed his hand to her stomach, pushing her into the mattress to still her. As his mouth did delicious things, he inserted one finger, and she could feel her muscles rippling around him.

"Christ," he murmured and eased his finger in and out of her in long, sensuous strokes that had her panting and begging for me. He wiggled his buried finger, and she could feel the tension rising in him as she grew slicker. She gripped the bed sheets and closed her eyes against the pleasure...so much pleasure.

"Yes," she whispered with effort.

His tongue found her clit as he inserted another finger, taking her higher and higher, but he didn't seem like he was in any hurry to push her over the edge. Instead, he burrowed his fingers, taking his sweet time with her. Honest to God, he was so different from the few college boys she'd been with. They were always in a hurry to get themselves off, paying little regard to her needs.

"You taste so good," he murmured from between her legs, and she went up on her elbows to see him.

He brushed the hot bundle of nerves inside her, and her body quaked as he slowly built her orgasm. Cripes, the man sure knew how to touch her. He made another slow pass with his tongue, and she became feverish with need. She writhed beneath him, her body shaking as he worked her into a state of aroused euphoria.

"Carter, please..."

He thumbed her clit, using slow, torturous circles that damn near drove her mad. Desire stirred deep between her legs, and soft quakes began at her core. His fingers plunged deeper, harder, and her hands went to her nipples to relieve the ache. He spent a long time between her legs, and she tossed her head from side to side, reveling in the erotic sensations. As if knowing she couldn't take any more, his mouth closed over her clit, his teeth scraping over the engorged nub. She gave a broken gasp, her body reacting to the increased pressure.

Her hips came off the bed, and her throat tightened as her body let go. Her sex muscles clenched around his fingers, and Carter's breath came in a labored rush.

"So good..." she murmured, a shudder ripping through her as an orgasm hit hard.

He stayed between her legs until she stopped quaking, then he climbed back up her body. His lips found hers.

"Josie," he whispered into her mouth, his kiss so full of

tenderness it made her breath catch. "Tell me you have a condom."

"I do," she whispered. "My nightstand."

Carter slid off her, and she touched his strong back as he sat on the edge of her bed and rustled around inside her nightstand. A second later, she heard the foil rip, and after rolling the condom on, he climbed back over her.

She widened her legs for him and his tip pressed against her opening. A tortured look crossed his face and he briefly closed his eyes. Once again, she thought he was about to change his mind, but when she lifted her hips and he slid in an inch, he let loose a growl and plunged inside.

She sucked in a sharp breath as he filled her. "Oh, God, Carter," she cried out. He stilled inside her and one hand went to her cheek.

"Josie," he murmured. "I'm sorry. I didn't mean..." He shook his head. "I just...I needed to be inside you so fucking bad...I couldn't slow—"

"Carter."

"Yeah."

"Zip it."

"Okay," he said and began moving, rocking into her. She lifted her hips and met each thrust. Moisture broke out on his forehead, and she brushed his hair from his face.

He shifted his body and his fingers burned her flesh as they raced over her, touching every inch of her like he couldn't get enough. His palm closed over one breast and he buried his mouth in her neck.

Her body tightened as he pumped deeper. In no time at all, the rippling waves of another orgasm took hold. Her whimper filled the room and Carter stilled inside her.

"I can't hold..." His breath came in a ragged burst. "I'm there," he murmured, and she held him tighter as he let go high inside her.

He collapsed on top of her, and she hugged him with her thighs, holding him inside. His breath was hot on her neck as he sucked in air.

"Jesus," he murmured. "I never came so fast before."

She hugged him tighter, loving the way he lost it with her. They stayed like that for a long time, until he grew flaccid. He slid out, discarded the condom, and fell back into bed beside her. Josie rolled into him and ran her fingers over his stomach, liking the way his muscles trembled beneath her touch.

Feeling content, she stretched and said, "Just for the record, Carter. I don't have many sleepovers."

"I know."

She went up onto her elbow to see him. "Oh, and how do you know that?"

His brow pulled together, and that same tortured look she was becoming familiar with returned. "Because you're so fucking sweet, Josie." He waved a finger back and forth between them. "Never once did you strike me as the kind of girl who took this kind of thing lightly."

"You're right. I don't."

He frowned, and emotions crept into his voice when he said, "You're the kind of girl who wants a family, kids, a future. I knew that the second I met you, which is why, before we started any of this, I told you I couldn't do more."

"I know. I get it. It was a onetime thing," she said, and while she thought she could be okay with that—not worrying about what tomorrow brought after a night with Carter—she wasn't so certain anymore. The sex had been so very sweet and tender, his every touch gentle and caring, that it tugged at her heart and drew her in that much deeper.

"We should probably get some sleep." He grabbed the blankets and pulled them over them. "I've got a long flight tomorrow."

As he crossed his arms behind his head and stared at her ceiling, there was something so lost and vulnerable about him it had her wanting to know more, *everything* about him.

"So you said you don't have any family waiting for you back home."

"That's right." He averted her gaze, but not before she caught the pain etched on his face.

She shifted and laid her head on his chest. He pulled one arm out from beneath his head and adjusted the blanket over her shoulders before wrapping his arm around her. It was a small gesture, but it made her feel so close to him.

"I tell you what, if you end up here for Christmas, you can share my family."

"Josie...I...why are you being so nice to me?"

She tipped her chin and found him looking at her. "Because I like you."

"Why? I mean, you know I let the casino deal go through, right? Even after your father asked me to stop it. Those people at the church aren't going to have a place to go, to eat."

She frowned. "You'll do the right thing."

"The deal is done. There is nothing I can do now."

She put her hand on his face and kissed him. "Christmas is a magical time, Carter. A time when wishes come true. All you have to do is believe."

"No, it's not," he said, his voice full of cynicism. He made a choking sound. "It's not that at all."

She caught the deep sadness in his eyes, and her heart ached for him. "Then what is it to you?"

"Nothing. It doesn't matter."

She rested her hand on his chest, and she could feel the powerful beating of his heart. "Maybe it matters to me."

His hand closed over hers. "I just don't like the holidays, okay?"

"Bad memories?"

"You could say that."

"Maybe we could make new ones, ones that make you feel—"

"That's just it. I don't want to feel."

"Carter?"

"Yeah."

"Maybe this year Santa will bring you what you want."

She listened to him scrub his chin. "I stopped asking for things fifteen years ago."

"What happened? Why did you stop asking?"

"Because every year I asked for the same thing. But a kid who is tossed around in the system because no one wants him never gets what he asks for."

"What did you want?"

His throat sounded tight when he swallowed. "I wanted the family I was placed with to keep me. Things were going so well. I was so happy. I was sure it was going to happen. So sure that, for the first time, I actually asked Santa for something else."

"What?"

"A dog."

"And instead of a family and a dog, you got moved?"

"Exactly." He snorted. "But I'm not complaining. I learned a few good lessons that year."

"Like what, that you should never ask anyone for anything?"

"Something like that." He went quiet for a long time then said, "I have no idea why I'm telling you any of this." He scoffed. "Maybe you're way better at interrogation than I am."

"No," she said, understanding what was really going on. "It's not me."

"If you tell me it's the white wolf, I'll—"

She rolled on top of him and wet her bottom lip. "You'll what?"

His ran his thumb over the seam of her lips. "I'll have to find a way to get you to zip it."

"I can think of a few ways," she whispered and closed her mouth over his.

16

Carter rebooked his flight and closed the laptop Josie had lent him earlier that morning. He took a sip of his coffee and watched her sway to a Christmas song as she wrapped a basketful of presents for her family. She tossed him a big smile, a smile so warm and sexy it had him reminiscing about everything they did in her bed the night before. He could feel his cock harden, wanting to drag her back to the bedroom for round two, even though he knew it was a bad idea. Last night never should have happened, but his body had been too fired up to think past the moment. Really, how could he be expected to think with any sort of clarity after glimpsing those sexy candy cane panties?

But seriously, he really should have kept his distance. She was a nice girl who needed a nice guy. What she didn't need was a prick who'd hardened himself to others and was about to put those less fortunate out on the street.

"All done," she said, and then started packing the presents back into the basket. "What time did you say your flight was?"

"Not until after dinner."

"Good, then we have plenty of time." She dashed to her room and came back wearing a knitted sweater. He looked at the dancing Christmas elf juggling three bulbs.

"Plenty of time for what? To sign up for the ugliest Christmas sweater contest?"

"Hey," she said, and tossed one at him. "I've got one for you, too."

He threw it back. "Like hell I'm wearing that."

"Come on, Carter. It's for the kids."

"How does that change things? I don't even like kids. I didn't even like myself when I was a kid." When she continued to stare at him, her lips all pouty and sexy, he gave an exaggerated exhaled. "Josie..."

She held the sweater up. "It's not so bad."

"How is it not so bad? It has a bucktoothed Rudolph on it."

"I know. Cute, isn't it? The kids love it. Jack has a bunch of them and won't mind you wearing this."

"How lucky for me."

"So that's a yes?"

He rubbed his temple and felt something in him give when he saw the way she was blinking up at him with those big, hopeful brown eyes. "Fine, but only because it's for the kids."

She gave him a knowing grin. "So you're saying you do like kids?"

He shook his head. "Just promise me no pictures. If this ever got out..."

"Then what? Others might see how adorable you really are?"

"Josie—"

"Come on, let's go."

He pulled the sweater on and cringed. This was so not going to be fun.

Thirty minutes later, he found himself at Stone Cliff resort, standing in the same boardroom where he and the mayor had faced off a couple of days ago. He looked over the huge stack of presents on the long table.

"Where did all these gifts come from?" he asked.

"My dad plays Santa and keeps track of what each child wants. He sets up a collection, and the locals donate money for toys. Stone Cliff matches the monetary donations, and my family, as well as my dad's staff, all go shopping."

Okay, he hadn't expected that. Something tugged at his chest. "Your father is a nice guy," he whispered to himself.

"Yeah, he is," she said quietly, a small, loving smile on her face.

"Hey, sis," a male voice called out from the doorway. "You ready to wrap?"

Carter turned. He saw two guys standing in the doorway holding tape, bags, and wrapping paper, and assumed they were Josie's brothers.

"Matt," Josie said, rushing to grab the stack of paper from him. "Please tell me you and Jason are here to help."

"Do we have to?" Matt's shoulders slouched. "You know we suck at this."

"Fine, then next year, you two can do all the cooking."

Matt looked at Carter and rolled his eyes. "Does she do that to you, too?"

"Do what?" Carter asked.

"Twist things until she gets her own way."

Josie whacked Matt. "Stop it. I do not do that."

"Oh yes, she does," Jason piped in. His gaze met Carter's and his lips quirked. "But I don't have to tell you that, judging from that sweater you're wearing."

When the two bothers laughed, there was nothing Carter could do but laugh along with them. "You're right, you don't have to tell me that."

She waved a dismissive hand at them all. "Matt, Jason. This is Carter. He's been staying at the cottage with me."

"So we heard," Matt said.

"Josie has been kind enough to lend me her sofa," Carter explained, although he suspected the two could see right through that lie. He might be a good lawyer with an unreadable poker face, but something told him everything that he and Josie had done last night was written all over them. "I'm catching the next flight east tonight."

"Well, as long as you're still here, you can help us wrap," Matt said, pulling a chair out.

Thankful for the distraction, Carter dropped down into one of the chairs and reached for the first box. The afternoon was lost to boxes and packages and listening to Josie and her brothers razz each other over the Christmas music being piped in through an overhead speaker. By the time he was done, late afternoon was upon them.

"One more stop before we deliver them," Josie said to Carter as he stood and stretched out his neck. "Then I'll take you to the airport."

"Okay," he agreed. He checked his phone, happy to see his flight was still on schedule. By this time tomorrow, he would be alone in his high-rise apartment, right where he wanted to be. Except, oddly enough, as he thought about leaving this Podunk town—Josie—a strange emptiness settled into his stomach. Then again, he hadn't eaten in awhile, so it could simply be hunger. Yeah, that's what it had to be.

Dinner hour was upon them when Josie pulled her vehicle into the driveway of a quaint bungalow. Decorated with lights and glitter and an inflatable Santa on the front lawn, he knew it had to be her folks' place. Shit. Had he known her "one more stop" would be here, he would have grabbed a cab and went straight to the airport.

"Why are we here?" he asked. "I thought we were taking the presents to the church."

"We will. I just have to stop here first. Come on."

"I'm pretty sure I'm the last guy your father wants to see, Josie."

"It's Christmas Eve, Carter," she said, like that explained everything.

She jumped from the truck and he followed her inside, where he was bombarded with everything Christmas. Mary greeted them at the door, and he glanced past her shoulders to see the dining room table all set for a family dinner.

He shifted from one foot to the other. He didn't belong here. "I probably should go."

"Don't be silly. Come in and make yourself at home," Mary said.

"What's this talk about leaving?" Mayor Walker asked as he stepped into the porch. "Get on in here and get warmed up, son."

Carter looked at Josie, who was shrugging out of her winter coat and chatting with her mother and Katee, the girl he saw kissing Jack at the church. He took a step back, ready to flee when her two brothers came in behind him, pushing him farther in to the house. With no way to escape, he just stood there, no idea what to do next.

Jack came around the corner with two glasses of eggnog. He handed one to Carter and in a conspiring manner, gestured with a nod. Carter looked up and saw the mistletoe.

"Thanks, man," Carter said, grateful that Jack had saved him from having to kiss Josie in front of her family...not that he would've minded kissing her again, but he assumed her father hated him enough already. Jack nudged him with his shoulder to set him in motion.

"You watch hockey, right?" Jack asked.

"Yeah."

"Good. Come on."

As he grabbed a chair and sipped his eggnog, Mayor Walker, Matt, and Jason joined them. Matt dug into a bowl of peanuts on the table as Josie disappeared into the kitchen with her mother and Katee. The guys all focused on the hockey game, and Carter looked around. With a big, decorated tree in the front window, the house was warm, lived in, the kind of house he would have killed to grow up in. His stomach clenched, and he tried desperately to push down the things he was feeling.

When a commercial break came on, Walker turned to him, and Carter hardened himself, expecting a confrontation. But once again, Walker surprised him with his fatherly concern.

"Josie said you've been having trouble getting out of town. I'm sorry to hear that. You must have family you're anxious to get back to see."

"Yeah," he said, hedging the truth.

"I guess if you have to be stuck anywhere for Christmas, Deerfield is just about as good as it gets."

It was easy to tell how much they all loved living here, and he couldn't blame them. Like one big happy family, the town all came together and did for one another—all one ever had to do was ask. He supposed Walker was right. If he had to be stuck somewhere, Deerfield was just about as good as it got.

"I don't plan on spending it here, actually." Carter glanced at his watch. "I leave in a few hours."

His father nodded. "That's too bad."

"I thought you'd be happy to see me on my way," Carter said.

"Not at all. As a matter of fact, this town could use a lawyer like you." He grinned and added, "On its side."

He wasn't sure whether it was a compliment or not, so he didn't say anything.

"But I guess you prefer the big city. Deerfield probably doesn't have enough to keep you here."

It has Josie...

Whoa...what the hell?

Before he had time to consider that, Mary called them from the dining room and everyone jumped to their feet. He followed Josie's brothers and her father into the room, and when he saw the big table set for seven, something inside him hitched.

Josie sat and tapped the seat beside her. "Come sit by me, Carter."

Carted lowered himself into the chair next to her, and Jack sat beside Katee, who looked at him with adoring eyes. Actually, she looked at him in much the same manner as Josie was looking at Carter. He swallowed. Hard.

Her father sat at the head of the table, and after everyone took a seat, Mary said a Christmas prayer and they all dug in. As soon as the plates were filled, everyone started chatting about their day, their jobs, the events that would take place later that night. Carter was constantly being pulled into the conversation, and the way everyone was so open, so welcoming, was totally messing with his head...and his heart.

The guys started in on Josie, telling Carter embarrassing stories from her childhood. She shot back with her own stories, and Carter couldn't help but smile at her feistiness. She really could hold her own against them all. As he dug into his mashed potatoes, he looked around the table and could feel the affection between siblings, parents.

God, what he would have done to be a part of this as a kid.

Soon, dinner was behind them, and after the dishes were washed and put away, they all piled into their cars and made their way to the church. Inside, they found numerous kids running around, excitedly waiting for Santa. Josie's father took center stage as Josie came in with a basketful of presents, her bothers and mother following behind. Carter hung back as the kids all lined up.

He folded his arms and watched each child take their turn on Walker's lap, and while he tried not to feel...there was nothing he could do to choke down his emotions. Josie helped her father dole out the presents, and every now and then, casted a glance his way. When the basket was empty and the kids were clutching their presents, Carter made a turn to go, deciding he'd wait in the SUV. Except Santa called out his name.

He stopped dead in his tracks and turned back. Surely there had to be another Carter in the crowd. Josie darted in the back room and came back with a box. She crooked her finger, and he shook his head. No way in hell was he about to go over there and sit on Santa's lap.

Jack came up to him and nudged him with his shoulder. "You'd better get over there." He looked at the Rudolph sweater than back at Carter's face. He grinned. "If you don't, she'll find a way to get you over there, and you might not like it."

Hating every second of this, he crossed the room and stepped up to Josie and her father. "You didn't have to get me anything."

Walker held the package out, and Carter's heart pinched as he thought about this family's generosity to strangers, how kind they were to him, despite the circumstances.

"It's Christmas, Carter," Walker said, like it meant something to him. And for the first time in his life, Carter couldn't help but think that maybe, just maybe, it did...

Something inside the box moved. "What the..."

"Careful," Josie said, and helped him balance it.

He pulled the lid off, and saw a big pair of brown, soulful eyes. Air left his lungs in a rush. He worked to breathe, to think, as tears pricked at his eyes. He pinched them shut and strived to pull himself together. Shit. He couldn't believe this was happening.

"Carter," Josie said, her voice low. "Are you okay?"

"Yeah," he said, even though he was pretty sure he'd never be okay again. The little puppy yelped, and Carter pulled it from the box. "Josie," he said. "You did this?"

"Well, you kept looking at him in the window, so I thought..."

Carter glanced around the room. He saw the young boy who'd asked Santa for a puppy and he turned back to Josie. "Thank you," he said. "I know he was meant for me, and I don't want you to think I'm not grateful, because I am, but I think there is someone who needs him more than I do."

She smiled. "That's what Christmas is all about, Carter."

Carter walked up to the little boy and handed him the puppy. As the boy's eyes lit up like a Christmas tree, his heart tightened. He turned to see the child's mother and the concern on her face.

"I have to leave town, but I need a place to board him," he explained. "I'll get your information from Josie so I can take care of his expenses."

When the mom smiled and thanked him, he knew he had to get out of there. This was all just too...much. He caught Josie's attention and pointed to his watch. She bounced over.

"Time to go?" she asked.

"Yeah."

They walked outside and he took note of the paw prints circling the truck. Feeling like he was being watched, a fine shiver moved through him as he glanced around, looking at the snow-covered sidewalks lit by the streetlamps. He fully expected to see a white wolf, but when his glance came up empty, he climbed in beside Josie. He stared out the window as she carefully negotiated the town's slippery streets.

Once they left the town center in their rearview mirror, Josie turned on the radio and sang along to the music as he watched the trees fly by. They rounded a corner and up ahead, he saw lights flashing and he leaned forward. "What's going on?"

"I don't know." Josie rolled her window down when they reached the police officer standing on the side of the road. "Hey Officer Sattler, what's up?"

"Highway is closed."

"You've got to be kidding me," Carter said.

"Why would I kid about that?" the officer asked as he ducked his head to look into the truck.

"I guess you wouldn't." Incredulous, Carter shook his head, even though he shouldn't have been surprised at the turn of events. "What's going on?"

Sattler pointed to the mountains hugging the road. "The snow started tumbling down onto the road. It's crazy. Nothing like that has ever happened around here before. It's going to take hours for the plows to clear it."

"Of course it is," Carter said, pushing back into his seat and calling up the next flight on his phone.

Josie looked at him. "Doesn't look like you're getting out of town tonight."

"Next flight is tomorrow mid-morning."

Office Sattler stepped back and signaled for Josie to do a U-turn on the road. She spun her vehicle around and shot him a glance. "Looks like you'll be here for Christmas after all."

"I think you knew that all along."

"Of course I did." She grinned. "Do you believe me now?"

"No," he said, even though there was a part of him that could no longer deny that something was going on. Either the town was conspiring against him, or the legend of the wolf was real, and he was here because he needed something.

"The wolf isn't finished with you yet."

He looked at Josie. She wet her bottom lip and his entire body came alive. The wolf might not be finished with him, but it was obvious he wasn't finished with her yet, either. When it came to her, there was a need he couldn't seem to assuage.

She went back to humming along to a song on the radio as she drove to her cottage in the mountains. Once inside, she took care of her dogs, then turned to him. "I'll be right back. I need to get in to my Christmas pajamas."

She disappeared, and remembering he still had on the bucktoothed Rudolph sweater, he pulled it over his head and tossed it onto the sofa instead of folding it neatly like he normally would. Josie came back into the main room, and he noticed the way she was staring at him, the way he was relaxing around her, letting down his guard.

Feeling out of sorts, he stood there looking at her and there was nothing he could do to rein in his emotions. He thought back to the way she'd lit up the church hall when she walked in. All eyes turned to her, but it wasn't because she was carrying an armload of presents. No, it was because she was kind, gentle, and sweet. In fact, she was like a damn burst of sunshine on a gray winter's day. She'd shared her family with him tonight. Invited him into her home where everyone treated him like he was one of their own. He knew she'd arranged the puppy, and that gesture meant so much to him.

As he thought about that, need ripped a hole in the shield around his heart. Josie was so sweet and generous it made him want to reevaluate his life and ask for things, even though he'd sworn a long time ago that he'd never ask anyone for anything.

"Are you okay?" she asked as he took in the nightgown decorated with sugarplums.

"Yeah," he answered, even though he wasn't. Christ, how

could he be falling in love with her? He barely knew her and they were completely different people.

With a sweet smile on her face, she went up onto her toes and pressed her lips to his.

"What was that for?" he asked.

"You made a little boy very happy tonight."

He shrugged. "What am I supposed to do with a puppy?"

"I don't know, but I can think of a few things you can do with me."

She stepped back and peeled off her nightgown. "I know you only said one time, but since you're stuck here with me, and it's Christmas, and this is kind of what I asked Santa for, I thought—"

"Josie," he said, his cock thickening as he gazed at her beautiful naked body.

"Yeah."

"Zip it," he said, pulling her into his arms. God, she was so perfect. Her hips were narrow, her breasts small, but it worked on her. Hell, everything worked on her. He was well past the point of denying that something was happening to him, something he had no control over, and this time, he knew it had nothing to do with the wolf and everything to do with the beautiful girl standing before him, offering him everything he'd always wanted but was too scared to ask for.

His mouth found hers and he scooped her up. He carried her to her room and tossed her onto the bed. "So is this what you asked Santa for?"

She nodded. "Yes."

"And you always get what you want because you're on the nice list, right?"

"Yes, but tonight I think I want to be naughty."

He groaned, ripped off his clothes, and climbed over her. He kissed her long and hard then grabbed a condom from her nightstand. He pushed into her and she opened so nicely for him. They held each other tight, like their lives depended on it as they came to orgasm, and once finished, he collapsed on top of her. She gave a contented sigh and he pulled her in tight. He held her for a long time, until her breathing changed.

As he listened to her soft sleeping sounds, he couldn't help but think sex was perfect with her. Heck, everything was perfect with her. Going over the events of the night, he pushed the covers off and stepped into the other room. The dogs looked at him, then rolled back over in front of the fire. He grabbed her laptop and booted it up. As it loaded, he went to work on making a pot of coffee because it was going to be a hell of a long night.

17

A streak of morning sunshine cut through the crack in her curtains and slanted against the wall, pulling Josie awake. She stretched and she reached for Carter only to find his side of the bed cold, too cold. She jackknifed up.

The smell of coffee and fresh burning wood in the hearth reached her nostrils. *He's still here!* She grabbed the top bed sheet, wrapped it around herself, and walked into the other room to find Carter at her computer.

She came up behind him and placed a kiss on his cheek. "Merry Christmas."

"Hey," he said, turning to face her, and the second she looked at him, her heart missed a beat. As his eyes moved over her face, she knew there was a new intimacy between them, one that went way beyond the physical. She also knew she'd gotten in over her head with him. He was leaving in a few short hours, and even though she wanted to ask him to stay, she knew it had to come from him. It had to be his decision.

"I'll be right back." She made a move to turn, to take care of her dogs, but Carter's hand on her wrist stopped her.

"I took care of them already."

"Oh," she said. "What are you doing up so early?"

"I'm not. I didn't go to bed yet."

She took in the dark circles under his eyes. "Why? What's going on?"

His breath came shallow and his voice seemed a bit shaky when he said, "You shared your family with me for Christmas, and I wanted to give you all something back." When she gave him a confused look, Carter spun the computer around so she could see it. As she leaned in to read, he explained, "I found the loop hole."

She quickly scanned the page. "Oh, my, God. The church is a heritage property." She jumped from her chair, and her bed sheet fell to the floor as she hugged him. "That means it can't be torn down!"

"Which means my client will no longer want it."

She clapped her hands. "You saved the church. I can't believe it. This is the best Christmas present ever. I need to call dad."

She made a move to go, but once again, Carter gripped her wrist to stop her. "I think you should wait."

"Wait? Why?"

"Something's come up."

"What?" She looked at the computer again then back at him.

"Me," he said, giving her a mischievous grin. God, she really did love this playful Carter.

"Oh," she said, taking note of the heat in his eyes as his gaze dropped to her breasts.

His mouth twitched. "That's what happens when you jump up and down naked, Josie."

Standing before him completely bare, she asked, "Is there something you want to ask me, Carter?"

Instead of answering, Carter stood and scooped her up.

As he carried her back to the bedroom, she thought about the changes in him in such a short time. Being here had done something to him, and she couldn't help but wonder if he'd board that plane and never look back, or if he'd finally open his mouth and ask her for what he wanted—needed.

●18

Carter adjusted his briefcase in his hand and walked through the relatively quiet airport, Josie keeping pace beside him. As they approached the billboard, he scanned it to find out his flight was still on.

He looked at Josie. "Doesn't seem like anything is keeping me here anymore."

She blinked up at him, and his heart missed a beat as he thought about how hard he'd fallen for her, how much he wanted her in his life. After spending the holidays with her and her family, he was second guessing everything he'd worked so hard for and reevaluating the direction of his life. Truthfully, he was hoping she'd ask him to stay, considering she was a girl who always asked for what she wanted. A knot tightened his stomach. Maybe she was ready for this to be over. Maybe it was only a Christmas fling for her. He supposed there was only one way for him to find out if there could be more between them. And that was to ask.

"Nope, looks like you're free to go," she said.

He raked his hands though his hair, his throat clenching hard. "Josie?"

"Yeah?"

He looked at the ticket counter, then back at her. He drew a deep breath and let it out slowly, knowing if he didn't do this, he would regret it for the rest of his lonely, unhappy life. Yeah, Josie was right about one thing. It wasn't natural for any animal to be alone. No matter how happy he'd thought he was, he really was miserable.

"I...I don't want to go," he said.

A smile touched her mouth. "No?"

"There's nothing back there for me. Not really."

"And there is something for you here in Deerfield?"

"I...I..."

She put her hand on his face and he closed his over it. "What is it?"

"I want to stay." He laughed. "Believe it or not, I kind of like it here."

"Even with all the reminders of Christmas?"

"Especially because of them. I kind of like the new memories we made."

"But you said you didn't want to feel."

He grinned. "I've discovered there are some things I really like feeling."

She returned his grin. "Yeah, there are some things I like you feeling, too."

He shrugged and looked around. "I could hang my sign here. I think your father was right. This town needs a good lawyer—on its side. Someone to help protect the town from vultures."

She laughed. "I think you're right."

"Josie."

Yeah?"

"If I stay, this thing between us..." He let his voice fall off.

She went still. Too still. And he worried that she might not want more. "Are you trying to ask me something, Carter?"

He took a deep breath and said, "Yes."

"Okay. Then ask."

After a long pause, he said, "If I stay, will you go out with me?"

"Of course." She laughed and hugged him. "All you had to do was ask, Carter. It's all you ever had to do."

"Okay then," he said, picking her up. She yelped and wrapped her arms around him. Everyone turned to look, but he didn't care. "Since I'm asking, can I take you home right now?"

"Yes."

"When we get there, can I take all your clothes off?"

"For sure."

Since he was on a roll, he continued, "Once I have you naked, can I kiss you all over?"

Heat moved into her eyes. "If that's what you want."

"It is. I also want to stay in bed with you until New Year's. Can we do that?"

She nodded. "New Year's sounds about right."

His throat tightened and all teasing was gone from his voice when he said, "I want to be with you Josie, and only you."

"I want the same."

"You do?"

"Yeah."

"Then why didn't you tell me?"

"Because you didn't ask."

He laughed out loud, then pressed his lips to hers. "What am I going to do with you?"

"Um, I believe you just laid out the perfect plan."

"Oh right." He grinned and hugged her tighter. "Let's get out of here then."

He carried her outside and set her down when they reached her SUV in the parking lot. Off in the distance, he heard a howl and turned toward the sound. His gaze met with a set of blue eyes against a white backdrop.

My white wolf.

"I guess it's true," he said. He looked at Josie, then back to the spot where the wolf had stood only seconds ago. He searched the area, but the animal was nowhere to be found.

"What's true?"

"The legend of the white wolf." He dropped another kiss onto her mouth and said, "What I wanted was not what I needed."

"I could have told you that."

"I suppose all I had to do was ask."

"Of course," she said laughing. "Now about this plan of yours..."

AFTERWORD

Thank you so much for reading, Love Lessons and Wrapped up. I hope you enjoyed the stories as much as I loved writing them. Keep reading for an excerpt of Single Dad Next Door. If you love boxed sets, check out FIREFIGHTER HEAT, and YOURS: Billionaire CEO series!

Interested in leaving a review? Please do! Reviews help readers connect with books that work for them. I appreciate all reviews, whether positive or negative.

Happy Reading,
   Cathryn

Rider

From my bar stool in Nelly's pub, I scoop my glass up from the long, oaken tabletop and hold it above my head in salute. "Here's to kicking ass and taking numbers," I say to my best friend, the man I call brother, despite the fact that our features are opposite in nearly every single way. Other than our height, and the fact that we both play in the NHL, Kane's longish hair is sun-drenched blond, whereas mine is dark and cropped short. His deep blue eyes have a way of catching the attention of everyone around him. Mine however, with a hint of metal gray, have been compared to an overcast day and help me blend into the background. Being invisible saved my ass a time or two in foster care.

"Here's to coming in first in our division," Kane says as he clinks glasses with me and jabs his thumb into his chest. "The Stanley Cup is coming home to Seattle with us this year, bro," he adds and I swallow half the bubbly soda in one gulp and slam my glass onto the bar top with more force than necessary. The bartender gives me a sideways glance and I grin at him before wiping my mouth with the back of my hand. I glance over my brother's shoulder and take stock of the crowded bar. In the near distance, the shrill of a woman's loud laugh swirls throughout the congested room and mingles with all the other blaring sounds.

Perfume reaches my nose, and as I feed off the energy in the crowd, I let it fuel my blood. I might be the guy to stand back and blend in, but deep down, I'm a total thrill-seeker. Last October however, shortly after the NHL season began, any kind of noise would have sent me to a dark corner drooling like a damn baby. Christ, that concussion really did a number on me. But it wasn't career-ending, and for that I'm grateful. Without hockey, I'm nothing.

"Where the fuck are the rest of the guys?" Kane asks and gestures for another shot.

I laugh but it has no humor. "It's Thursday. Where the fuck do you think they are?" Christ, except for a handful of the guys, most on the team are married with kids, and those who live in Seattle are home snuggled in with their loved ones on this rainy Thursday night. The others are likely holed up in their hotel rooms skyping and babbling shit about missing home. A sound crawls out of my throat, a half laugh, half snort. It's not that I'm jealous of their relationships, or anything. Nope, I'm a bachelor for life, and not fucking jealous at all.

Or much, anyway.

"Right. Pussies," Kane says, his voice a bit slurred. A couple shots of rum will do that to a guy. We have a game in two days, and while Kane can put the booze back as well as the next guy, and still be on top of his game, for me...not so much. I'm not about to risk anything when it comes to hockey. It's all or nothing for me. And I'll only settle for all.

I turn, lean against the bar, and scan the establishment a second time. "We have a live one," I say when I catch sight of the pretty redhead coming from the hallway. She presses her lips together, smoothing her freshly applied color, and runs her hands through her thick, wavy hair. I'm good at reading body language, a must on the ice, and if those gestures aren't a sign that she's open for suggestions, I don't know what is. "Two o'clock," I say and Kane spins on his stool.

"She's gorgeous," he says and I grin when his jaw drops.

I nudge Kane with my shoulder. "Do I know how to pick them for you, or what?"

"You sure you don't want this one? I know you have a thing for redheads."

"Nah. I'm just going to finish my soda and head home. I have some shows to catch up on."

Kane shakes his head and I brace for the lecture. "Are you seriously still watching The Handmaid's Tale?"

"Shut the fuck up, and it wouldn't hurt you to watch something other than sports once in a while."

"Man, you need to get laid more than I thought." He finishes off his drink. "Go ahead. You take this one."

As the girl approaches, I push off the counter and step in front of her. "So I was thinking..." I begin, and she stops abruptly and stares at me with pretty green eyes.

"About?" Her dark lashes fall slowly as her gaze pans the length of me. While she doesn't yet know it, her leisurely inspection of my body is a waste of time. It's not me she's going home with tonight.

"Well, I was thinking about asking for your number." Before I continue, I cringe, and suck in air like I have something nasty on my tongue. "But I have this thing..."

Her eyes narrow in on me. "You have a *thing*?" she asks, and the fact that she's playing along lets me know she's open to a hook-up.

"Yeah, the doctors are calling it a third nipple." I lower my voice and add, "For now, anyway." Kane chuckles as the girl's eyes widen. "More tests need to be done, of course."

She takes a small step backward, like she might catch what I have. "Ah, why are you telling me this?"

I move to the side to make room for my bro, and right on cue, Kane stands. Her gaze shifts, and appreciatively takes in my brother. "Because this guy only has two nipples. You seem like a girl who would appreciate that, plus he told me you were the most beautiful woman in the room."

"He did?" A smile curls up the corners of her mouth, and I inch back even more, biting back my grin as the two begin talking.

And that, ladies and gentlemen, is how to be a good wingman. Not that Kane really needs one, but we have fun playing the game.

Since my job here is done, I plop back down onto my stool and let Kane work his magic. I hang for a bit until Kane pulls his car keys from his pocket and hands them to me.

"Get my car home, bro. We're taking an Uber."

"You got it," I say and finish my soda. I grin at my buddy. "Have fun."

"Take your own advice, why don't you." He stares at me for a moment, like he's truly concerned about my well-being, and I wave my hand to shove him off. He opens his mouth and I snort, turning from him to let him know it's not a conversation we're having. Once he steps away, I angle my head and watch them walk from the bar. When he disappears outside, I pull my phone from my pocket and check the hour. Damn, I put that hook-up together in record time. I'm getting better and better at this shit, and if I hurry, I might be able to catch up on two episodes before I crash.

I grab my glass, about to take my last sip of cola before I head out, when the sound of hands clapping reach my ears. I turn to find a girl nodding and applauding me.

I grin at her. "You liked that, did you?" I ask, as I take in her clear skin, sharp brown eyes that are twinkling with amusement, and dark hair tied back in a ponytail. My gaze drops to her loose-fitting scrubs.

"Yeah, well played. Does your charm only work on girls, or does it work on guys too?"

I arch a brow and cock my head as my gaze moves over her make-up free face. Not that she needs paint. She has that whole girl-next-door thing going on and it really works for her. "You don't strike me as the kind of girl looking for a hook-up."

She gives a very unladylike snort as I finish my last gulp of soda. "What?" She tugs on her hair. "Is it the ponytail, or the fact that I'm not showing my tits?"

Her retort catches me off guard and I nearly choke on my drink as my gaze drops to her chest. "Uh, yeah," I say, instantly liking her. The truth is, women approach me all the time, and while I seem to have an instant rapport with this one, and there's an undeniable spark between us, she didn't come over here to get me between her sheets and no way is she really looking for me to be her wingman. So, what does she want?

She laughs at that. "At least you're honest." Dark eyes full of curiosity and playfulness narrow in on me, but behind those dark lashes I sense her cautiousness. "What else gave me away?"

"You're dressed in scrubs."

She shrugs. "I'm a nurse at Seattle General. I came here straight from work to meet a friend for drinks."

"You have freckles," I say, that observation coming out of nowhere and catching her off guard.

She crinkles her nose. "Yeah, I know. They're awful."

"I never said they were awful."

She rolls her eyes like she doesn't believe me. "Well, you have a dimple."

I poke my finger into my right cheek. "Wait, you say that like it's a bad thing?"

She sighs. "It's not."

I lean toward her conspiratorially. "I'm a nice guy, and because I am, I'm going to give you a warning. If you look at it too long, you'll be forever charmed."

"Oh, my God. Are you for real?"

"Sadly yes," I say, and she laughs with me. I glance around. "Where's this friend you're having drinks with? Is she going to hate me for keeping you captive with my dimple?"

"Ah, nope." She casts a sad glance at the door. "She kind of left with your friend."

Oh shit. "Ah, sorry about that."

"Yeah, that was Lindsay. My best friend."

"And now I'm responsible for you drinking by yourself?"

"I'm done drinking. I have a shift tomorrow." She glances around. "She's safe with your friend, right?"

"Absolutely. Kane is one of the good guys."

She nods. "Okay, so I really am curious. Do your lines only work only on women, or do they work on guys too?"

I gesture for the bartender for two more sodas. "Want to find out?"

"Sure. It's not like I have anything better to do."

"Okay. What's your type?"

"You know, the typical, tall dark and handsome." She holds her hand out. "I'm Jules, by the way. You should probably know that much if you're going to be my wingman."

"Rider," I say and take her soft hand in to mine. Damn, her hands are so tiny. Much like the rest of her. After a quick shake, I scan the bar. "What about that guy there?"

"Too much hair gel," she says. "If he moved in for a kiss, it might put my eye out."

I grin. "Okay, what about that one?"

She crinkles her nose. "He hasn't looked up from his phone all night."

"Yeah, he'd probably want you to send boob picture or something." I eye her teasingly. "Wait, are you into that? Asking for a friend."

She laughs and whacks me. "No."

"What about him?" I spot a nice-looking guy—hey, I'm man enough to admit when a guy is good looking—cuts across the floor, his gaze locked on the bartender, and from the interest in his eyes, I'm not certain it's a drink he wants from the man. Nothing wrong with that, but if she's interested, it's still not going to stop me from being a good wingman.

"Yeah, he's kind of cute."

I stand, and cut him off. "Hey, bud," I begin. "I've got to get out of here." I jerk my thumb toward Jules. "I don't want to leave my friend Jules alone." The dude looks around my shoulder to take in Jules as she twists on the stool. "We're just friends because she's not my type."

Recognition flashes in the guy's eyes when they stray back to me. "Wait, aren't you—?" he begins, and I cut him off by holding my hands in front of myself, like I'm about to cup two perfect breasts. I get it, he's a fan, and while I'm always up for a picture or an autograph, I don't want to switch gears right now. I realize I'm loved because of hockey, but I guess I just want to be me right now. Not that anyone loves that guy.

"Her tits you know. They're way too big. I'm a mouthful kind of guy."

Jules squeals in horror behind me, and I bite back a grin as the dude stares at me like I'm a serial killer trying to lure him to my basement with the help of my girlfriend. He gestures with a nod to the group of guys behind him. "Uh, yeah, I have to go."

Jules and I burst out laughing as he zig-zags through the

crowd and meets up with his friends. They huddle and cast suspicious glances our way. Maybe it's time for us to vacate the place. I reserve my fighting for the rink.

Jules gives a slow shake of her head. "You've got no game, Rider."

"Hey, I've got game," I say, feigning offense. "That guy was just more interested in the bartender. Let me try again," I say, although oddly enough, I've lost the desire to hook her up with some random guy.

She gives me a dubious look, stands, and shoves me. "Move aside, rookie. Let me show you how it's done." She scans the room. "What's your type? And yeah, I get it. You don't like big breasts."

"I never said that," I counter as I try to judge the size of hers, but they're hidden so well behind her scrubs I can't tell. "I like *all* breasts."

She puckers her lips. "I bet you do."

"Yeah. I do," I admit and she shakes her head. "What can I say? I'm honest to a fault." When she rolls her eyes, I say, "I like women, Jules. Tall, short, thin, plump. You name it."

"Hair color?"

I glance at her ponytail. "As long as I can tug it, it doesn't matter what color it is."

As soon as the words leave my mouth, her lips part, and wait...was that a fast intake of breath I just heard? I study her closely, examine the fresh flush on her face. Funny, others might find her plain, but the more time I spend with her, the cuter I find those freckles, and the sexier I find everything about her—including her scrubs. I can't even blame it on alcohol since I'm dry tonight. Yeah, okay, maybe Kane was right. I need to get laid more often.

"Did I embarrass you?" I ask.

"No," she says, with a quick jerk of her head.

I part my legs on the stool and since I value my nuts, I

resist the urge to pull her between them. "Then why are your cheeks red?"

She lets out an exasperated breath. "Do you say everything that pops into your brain?"

"Pretty much." My gaze moves over her pretty pink cheeks. "Oh, wait, maybe you're not embarrassed. Maybe you're arous—"

"So you don't have a type," she blurts out, cutting me off. "How about the one coming toward you right now. Twelve o'clock."

I look the pretty girl over. Perfect hair. Perfect makeup. Perfect clothes. "She seems very high maintenance."

"Yeah, I think you might be right."

"Hmmm, what about that one?" she says and I follow the direction she's pointing.

I give a slow shake of my head. "Nope, she's downing her drinks like she fears there's going to be an alcohol shortage."

"What about her friend?"

I study her body language for a second. "See the way she's scanning the place, her hands braced by her sides?"

"Yeah," she says.

"I'm pretty sure she fears we're about to face a zombie apocalypse."

Jules laughs out loud and when it dies off, she says, "What about the one coming right at you."

I reluctantly tear my gaze from Jules and make eye contact with the blonde. I stiffen. Shit. I know where this is going, and I'm not in the mood—not when I've been having a good time here.

"What's wrong?" Jules asks.

"Nothing," I lie.

"I thought that was you, Rider," the girl says, and puts her hands on my chest as she juts one hip out in a suggestive manner.

"Do I know you?" While I might not know her, I know her type, and I know what she's after. But what's really bugging me is Jules and I were having fun, and I wasn't ready for that to end. Honestly, I haven't laughed or joked like that with a woman in…ever.

The blonde gives a breathless laugh. "Not yet." She runs her finger down my chest. "I'm Candy, by the way."

"Of course you are," I say.

"Want to get out of here? Go back to my place, or yours if you prefer."

Wow, how fucking rude to act like Jules doesn't even exist. Sure, she's not the kind of girl usually found on my arm, but still.

"Candy, this is Jules. My fiancée." I tap my leg, a gesture for Jules to take a seat.

Without even missing a beat, Jules takes my cue, sidles closer to me, and extends her hand. "Candy, it's nice to meet you." Goddammit, a woman with beauty and brains. If I weren't a one-night kind of guy, I'd hang on tight to this one. But I'm not into tomorrows, so that's a stupid thought.

Candy falters and stares at Jules' hand like it's about to grow a head and bite her.

"Yeah right," she fires back, her eyes narrowing as her head bobs back and forth between the two of us.

"Why is that so hard to believe?" Jules asks in a voice so sultry and smooth it could churn butter.

Candy's head jerks back, her lips pursed so tight they're beginning to turn white. "Rider Lewis, the NHL's best wing-man, does not date, or do commitments. Everyone knows that."

In a move that displays possession, Jules settles between my spread legs and sets her sweet ass down on my left thigh.

She blinks innocently at Candy. "I guess I must have missed the memo."

Hands On

Hands On

Body Contact

Full Exposure

Dossier

Private Reserve

House Rules

Under Pressure

Big Catch

Brazilian Fantasy

Improper Proposal

Boys of Beachville

Good at Being Bad

Igniting the Bad Boy

Bad Girl Therapy

Stone Cliff Series:

Crashing Down

Wasted Summer

Love Lessons

Wrapped Up

Eternal Pleasure Series

Instinctive

Impulsive

Indulgent

Sun Stroked Series

Seaside Seduction

Deep Desire

Private Pleasure

Captured and Claimed Series:

Yours to Take

Yours to Teach

Yours to Keep

Firefighter Heat Series

Fever

Siren

Flash Fire

Playing For Keeps Series

Slow Ride

Wild Ride

Sweet Ride

Breaking the Rules:

Hold Me Down Hard

Pin Me Up Proper

Tie Me Down Tight

Stand Alone Title:

Hands on with the CEO

Torn Between Two Brothers

Holiday Spirit

Unleashed

Knocking on Demon's Door

Web of Desire

ABOUT CATHRYN

New York Times and *USA today* Bestselling author, Cathryn is a wife, mom, sister, daughter, and friend. She loves dogs, sunny weather, anything chocolate (she never says no to a brownie) pizza and red wine. She has two teenagers who keep her busy with their never ending activities, and a husband who is convinced he can turn her into a mixed martial arts fan. Cathryn can never find balance in her life, is always trying to find time to go to the gym, can never keep up with emails, Facebook or Twitter and tries to write page-turning books that her readers will love.

Connect with Cathryn:
Newsletter https://app.mailerlite.com/webforms/landing/c1f8n1
Twitter: https://twitter.com/writercatfox
Facebook: https://www.facebook.com/AuthorCathrynFox?ref=hl
Blog: http://cathrynfox.com/blog/
Goodreads: https://www.goodreads.com/author/show/91799.Cathryn_Fox

Pinterest http://www.pinterest.com/catkalen/

www.ingramcontent.com/pod-product-compliance
Lightning Source LLC
Chambersburg PA
CBHW021150190726
48288CB00008B/2915